COBY THINKS

The Path of an Heir

Legends of Ardenia: The Cursed Land - Book One

Copyright © 2024 by Coby Thinks

All rights reserved. No part of this publication may be reproduced, stored or transmitted in any form or by any means, electronic, mechanical, photocopying, recording, scanning, or otherwise without written permission from the publisher. It is illegal to copy this book, post it to a website, or distribute it by any other means without permission.

This novel is entirely a work of fiction. The names, characters and incidents portrayed in it are the work of the author's imagination. Any resemblance to actual persons, living or dead, events or localities is entirely coincidental.

Coby Thinks asserts the moral right to be identified as the author of this work.

Coby Thinks has no responsibility for the persistence or accuracy of URLs for external or third-party Internet Websites referred to in this publication and does not guarantee that any content on such Websites is, or will remain, accurate or appropriate.

First edition

This book was professionally typeset on Reedsy.
Find out more at reedsy.com

Dedicated to Melissa FREAKING Fisher - thank you for being part of my life, even if it was only for a few years playing high school lacrosse. I hope wherever you are now, you're doing well.

Readers: This story contains themes of fantasy violence, anxiety/paranoia, mild swearing, sexism, and transphobia/misgendering. Target audience is 17+ Please take this into account before reading.

Contents

Foreword	ii
Maps	iii
Prologue	1
1 Histories	10
2 Swords and Soldiers	27
3 Fairy Tales	38
4 The Festival	50
5 Ifs and Buts	64
6 The Truth	75
7 Trust	87
8 Escape	98
9 Men and Monsters	113
10 Kindling	124
11 Campfire Stories	136
12 Welcome to Stonewell	151
13 Blessings	162
14 Superstitions	173
15 Snowfall	189
16 Bloodshed	200
17 Trust: Broken	214
Glossary	227
Acknowledgments	229
About the Author	231

Foreword

Inside this book you'll find just one of the magical tales which take place in a land called Ardenia. A region otherwise known as The Land of Three Castles.

The castle of focus in *this* story is the castle in Cidon, the central kingdom. Some other time, I may tell you tales of the isolated desert kingdom of Ashan in the south, or perhaps some other time I'll tell you the tales that take place in the timber woods and snow plains of Rasnia in the north.

Not to say that only one castle matters for this story, because that could never be true. But this time, for this story, the people of note started off in the center. The humid land of lakes and armies that Cidon was, at the time this story came to pass.

This story, as fantastical as it is, even those like yourselves in the most far-off dimensions can understand. Magic and all that might be hard to believe for you, but this story is first and foremost about people. People are the same everywhere you look, and as easy as breathing to understand.

As long as you open your eyes, that is.

Maps

Map of Cidon

World Map

Prologue

Year 1395 of The Ages of Old - or - Year 1 of The Age of Sleeping Dragons

The air was humid and stale all at once. Thick, almost foggy with the moisture of rainwater leaking down through the rocks - but tasteless and old, with the fact that nobody but the two of them had entered these caves for a very long time.

Cassandra tightened the grip on her brother's hand, pulling him close as they picked their way through tunnels and caverns.

They were familiar to her, or they had been once. She'd grown up in these mountains, but with the queen's aspirations and the friendship they'd had, Cassandra had taken Walter and left to join her in the lower valleys.

Now it was time to go home, and these caves were safer to travel through than the roads and canyons above ground.

"What was that?" Walter's head whipped around, knocking into her elbow, and Cassandra sighed softly.

"Just rocks and water." She couldn't blame him for being nervous. The past few months had been nerve-wracking for even her, and she wasn't a child like him. "Stay close, we'll be alright."

"I heard something," he insisted in a whisper, hanging heavier onto her arm, making her shoulder ache. "Do you think they found us?"

"No, Walter, they won't find us." Even the idea of it made her stall, turning to look behind them into the darkness of the tunnels. The other hand she had out, unburdened by Walter's hold, glowed as faintly as she could make it even though only a handful of people even *knew* about these caves.

That handful had split in two, and the other half was made up of the people they were running from. If Eleanor couldn't talk the queen into reason, it was entirely possible that someone would come through searching for them.

"See?" Even in the silence, and absence of movement, Walter flinched back, hiding behind her again from the caves they'd just walked through. "I don't want them to find us, Cass, I'm scared!"

"It's fi-" There was a clattering of stone in the darkness, of rocks being tripped over and feet dragging momentarily, and Cassandra clamped her mouth shut.

No... it must be some kind of animal or a coincidence. How could someone have found them *already*? They'd gotten a few *days* head start, and they'd only been running for a little over a week.

"Make a light, Walter," She pushed him back a few steps, not taking her eyes from the direction of the sound. "Can you do that?"

He nodded wordlessly, lifting a hand to rub the fingers together until he'd managed to replicate the spell she'd been holding for a few hours now.

"Take this," she slung the bag off her shoulder onto his, then ruffled his hair. "Go for as many steps as you can count, and then wait for me there."

"Wh- no! I don't want to leave you." His eyes widened in the pale light, and Cassandra grimaced. "What if something happens?"

"I'll call for you if I need you, I'll be fine." The queen was too vain these days to come into a dirty cave by herself, so it must be some soldier or hired hand. If it was the queen, Cassandra wouldn't have a chance... but if it were anyone else it was possible to defeat them.

Walter was too young for all that, so she had to get him to go on without her.

"But-"

"No buts." She poked him on the nose with one glowing finger, earning a worried smile. "Everything will be alright, Walter. I'll see you soon, get going."

He wouldn't be too far... he couldn't count all that high, even if he *was* a magical prodigy. She'd put some distance between them by backtracking, but getting him out of harm's way by no means meant getting him lost in these caves. He'd been far younger than he was now, when they left, and he didn't have them memorized the way she did.

With a kiss on his forehead and a tight hug around her waist, Cassandra finally convinced Walter to keep on through the tunnels without her.

Cassandra turned back the way they'd come, holding her hand out and stepping forward as quietly as she could, squinting into the darkness for whatever had made the sound.

Another rustle, dragging movement on stone, and there was a spark of hope in her chest that it was just an animal of some kind that had followed them down here when she pulled the covering from the entrance.

Then a glitter of green light, magic that was as familiar to her as her own, made Cassandra's stomach twist.

Eleanor was one of the few people in Ardenia who could

have found them this quickly, being one of the most powerful seers alive. Add that in with her experiments on teleportation magic, and...

Another step forward illuminated blood on the stone.

Every circumstance of their parting seemed to rush from Cassandra's mind, seeing the figure of someone who had been her friend for years slumped against the wall. Eleanor took another dragged step forward, more blood gushing from the wound in her stomach as she did so.

"Oh, *stars...*" Cassandra pushed forward, catching her before she could fall only to lower Eleanor down onto the ground as gently as she could. "What happened? Who did this? I..."

Was she alone? Was this a trap? Had Cassandra just gotten herself and Walter both killed because she forgot, for only a moment, that Eleanor had betrayed them to stay with the queen? Did it even matter, with her oldest friend in the world dying at her fingertips?

"I *tried*," Eleanor rasped. Her eyes still glowed their bright green, and the magic in the air around her was staining bits of her skin green beneath the blood.

The tunnel was empty save for the two of them, and the dimming light of Walter walking away, counting in a whisper with every step.

"Hold on, I can fix this." Cassandra swallowed the fear back, pressing two hands down on the wound as best she could.

She was no healer, nor a medical witch, but she'd been in enough tight spots that she knew magic could seal wounds if she focused enough.

That was proving difficult, though, thoughts spinning in confusion as to why Eleanor was here, injured. Why was she here alone? Who'd hurt her so badly that she could hardly walk or speak?

"Just sit still, stay awake." Cassandra cleared her throat. "Who *did* this?"

"I couldn't stop her," Eleanor whimpered, face twisted in pain while the magic tried and failed to close her wound.

Oh, she needed to focus or Eleanor was going to die right here under her hands.

"Who?" Cassandra asked distractedly, though something deep in her soul already knew.

"Nadia."

The queen.

Of course it had been the queen. If Eleanor had tried to stop her from doing anything... Well, there was a reason Cassandra had abandoned the capital and taken Walter someplace far away from there. The queen had become twisted with power, believing herself to be a god, and Cassandra hadn't even dared to confront her - instead running away, taking Walter to these mountains, which she could only hope were safe.

Eleanor was another story. She'd always had a bit more sway when it came to Nadia, but... but *this* only showed that the queen was beyond convincing.

"I loved her," Eleanor's eyes were glassy, staring up at the dark ceiling of the cave. Cassandra bit into her own tongue, tasting blood, and pulled more energy up into her hands to try the healing spell again. "I thought... I could stop her. But I couldn't and now she's..."

"Just breathe, Eleanor." Cassandra grit out, relieved to feel the skin stitch itself back together under her touch. "We can talk later, we can-"

"It doesn't matter." Oh, she'd never heard Eleanor sound so defeated. "It's too late."

Her eyes still shone green light, which meant that despite her injuries, Eleanor was still using her abilities to see somewhere different.

Or some*when*.

She'd gotten into the nasty habit of living in her visions, rather than the present, and Cassandra could only hold onto the hope that they still had a bit of time before whatever this was really happened.

"Walter!" With the wound mostly closed, she cleared her throat and yelled back over her shoulder. "Walter, come here, please! Bring the bag- I need bandages."

They only had a small supply of such things, but for this...

No matter how they felt, or what Eleanor had done in the recent past, Cassandra needed her alive if she wanted to know what it was that she'd tried to stop. And... they had been very good friends, once, hadn't they?

"Cass! Are you-" Walter's steps skidded to a halt behind her. "Is that *Ellie*?"

"Bandages, Walter, we can talk once I know she's alright." Cassandra pushed another round of healing magic through her hands, but it was weaker than the first. She'd been creating light all morning, and the first successful push had taken a lot out of her.

Wincing as the contents of their bag were dumped unceremoniously on the dirt, Cassandra accepted the rolls of bandages that Walter found when he dug through the pile. They could repack later, once this was... anything other than what it was right now.

It got there, slowly, with bandages wrapped around Eleanor's torso and Walter's light illuminating her work. After a few more minutes, Cassandra was almost sure that the wounds would no longer be fatal.

Eleanor was still pale and shaking, and still stuck in her visions as they propped her against the tunnel wall and gave her water.

"I'm sorry," she mumbled deliriously as Cassandra helped her stand, walking her and Walter both toward a bigger section of the caves where they could stay more comfortably. "I tried, I tried…"

"I know you tried." Cassandra could only imagine what Eleanor must have said to the queen to get such a violent reaction. Then again, they both knew what the queen was capable of.

"Here, sit here Ellie!" Walter, the sweet child he was, had run ahead and laid out his blankets and bedroll in a flat bit of the cavern floor. "Is it gonna be okay, Cassandra?"

"She'll live." Cassandra knew that wasn't the answer to his question, but she lowered Eleanor down and helped her sit. "I need you to talk to me, Eleanor. Focus on me, stop looking at other things."

Finally, the green light dimmed and Eleanor looked like she might cry.

Cassandra could count on one hand the times she'd seen the other cry. Oh, this… this was not good, was it?

"This is all my fault," she whispered, one hand curling over the bandages on her stomach. "I-"

"It's not. Whatever it is… it's not."

"I thought I could stop her, I thought she would *listen* to me." Eleanor rambled, voice cracking. "But I only made it worse, and now…"

"Now…?" Cassandra almost didn't want to know. "What is she going to do, Eleanor?"

"She's already done it." Even as she spoke, Eleanor's brow furrowed in confusion. "Or... or she will soon. Oh, stars, I'm not sure anymore."

Either way, they'd learned the hard way that if Eleanor saw something in a vision, nothing could stop it from happening. All they could do was brace for it because trying to stop the future from taking place would never work.

"What is it, Ellie?" Walter held out his canteen of water to her, but Eleanor didn't seem to see or hear him. Her eyes had started to shine once again, and Cassandra wasn't sure how to pull her out of this spiral without hurting her - which right now, she couldn't *take*.

"What's she doing?" She asked, defeated, and Eleanor's entire body seemed to shudder with the force of the vision.

"She's furious. They're trying to stop her, we- they- she doesn't want to be stopped. She wants them to *hurt*."

All Cassandra could do was listen, while Eleanor outlined her vision in a trembling voice. A powerful circle of runes, etched into standing stones somewhere in the forests of Cidon. Bodies, and live sacrifices, which no self-respecting caster would ever use in their spells.

Queen Nadia had lost any respect she'd once earned, when she decided she would be a god.

"There's a curse," Eleanor whispered hoarsely. "On all of us- all of Ardenia... from the northern coasts to the deserts."

"That's-" Cassandra wanted to say it was impossible. *It should be impossible.*

If anyone could do the impossible... it would be the queen.

Then Eleanor's voice shook, shifting, until they were hearing an entirely different voice, speaking the words to a damned, powerful incantation.

"For the pain I've suffered at your hands-"

That was rich. Who'd gotten close enough to hurt her without becoming a dead man? Almost nobody, except maybe the three of them sitting here.

"I lay a curse upon this land."

'This land' was vague... Cassandra could only hope that would weaken the curse.

"For promises you didn't keep, I put all the greater beasts to sleep."

An ambitious spell... but from the ritual Eleanor had described, Cassandra wasn't positive if it was impossible or not.

"No magic here will grow or change, the gifted ones my fury face."

That could mean anything. Cassandra frowned nervously, only hanging onto the fact that *every* spell had an end, natural or planned, and the queen knew that just as well as the rest of them.

"No knight or prince can change a thing - you can only be saved by the daughter of a king."

1

Histories

Year 299 of the Age of Sleeping Dragons

History was an odd thing - or at least, the study of it was. Delving into times and places other than this one, surrounded by the smell of paper and ink in the library, it was one of the very few places one could feel truly at peace. In another life, Nadia thought she might have been a scholar like her friend Jasper. Though if Nadia could choose her life, she would change a lot.

For one, she would have named herself 'Nadia' off the bat and she wouldn't carry the title of 'Prince' either. She would be Princess Nadia, heir to the throne, rather than Prince Lewis.

She *had* to be Prince Lewis. That was how the world saw her, but at least in her own head, she could be Nadia.

In her own head, in a library in the castle where even her best friend didn't know her true thoughts. Jasper had no idea how she'd stared at noblewomen all her life, wishing she could be as pretty and graceful as they were. Even thinking it felt silly, Nadia couldn't imagine how it would sound to *say* it. He was the smartest person she knew, sitting across the table now and hunched over his transcription work, and Nadia considered herself lucky to even know him.

He was good company, with his tendency to ramble Nadia was able to sit and listen, instead of being the focus of a room like she was in her tutoring and training sessions. He was a good model, too, when she tired of sketching landscapes and portraits of herself that always looked *wrong*. Even he, most likely, would laugh at her for wanting to be born differently than she had been.

Nadia couldn't change her birth, which was as much history at this point as any old ruler, war, or trade deal she could study in the scrolls and journals in their library. That was actually where she'd come across the name she chose for herself when she wanted one other than Lewis.

She'd been throwing herself into the oldest of their records, desperate for anything to distract herself from the uncomfortable present, when she'd come across scrolls that had been lost in the back of a shelf and forgotten about. The contents were in regards to a ruler of Cidon that was only briefly mentioned in any other records, and it had been a welcome source of fascination for a few years now.

'Nadia' was the name of a queen who had ruled three centuries earlier, before being usurped by the late King Arthur. Arthur Dolloway himself was the start of the royal bloodline that led to her Father, and he'd lived and led through a long era of peace, strengthening the borders and the agriculture of Cidon.

King Richard took a different approach to ruling than that, with his dedication to defense, and combat, and war.

All Nadia really knew about war was the history of them in Ardenia and the difficult training she'd been trying to get a hang of for a few years now. It was *much* easier to read about old things than it was to understand the bad parts of the world now, while they were still happening. She did her best to study old wars, though, seeing as she would have to know enough to lead Cidon someday and assist the other kingdoms of Ardenia in anything similar to what was happening now.

The thing Nadia most enjoyed to study was the old records - to try and find the stories of the queen she'd named herself after, even if it was only for herself. It was nice to lose herself in stories so old they would never truly impact her life, and it was a reprieve from being a prince that Nadia took advantage of far too often.

Jasper loved history even more than she did, *and* he was much better at remembering everything important, and he said it was likely that the old Queen Nadia just hadn't valued the art of keeping records.

Nadia was infinitely intrigued by the idea of a queen with no king - when all records of Cidon's queens other than her had been second to the name of their husband.

So, if there was any queen Nadia would model herself after, it would be that one. Her mother had died too young to have much history, and most others were footnotes. But Queen Nadia - some passages that *had* survived the centuries even called her 'Nadia the Great' - *she* was something interesting. That was one reason Nadia even chose the name.

Not that anybody else knew that.

All anyone else knew, and that was really only a few people, was that *Prince Lewis* was just very interested in old history. Not even Jasper knew that Nadia was *Nadia*, and he was her best friend in the world.

Jasper... Jasper was one thing that made being the heir -

being *Prince Lewis* - worth it at all. He'd moved to the castle when they were children, sent early to become a scholar and a scribe. Now he was one of the youngest to graduate past apprenticeship, and he was a welcome constant in the library.

The library was a cramped room of shelves and desks, almost always bustling with one or two scholars or scribes, and Nadia found herself going there to read or draw when she wasn't attending any of her general lessons in swordsmanship, diplomacy, economics… everything she'd need to be a good ruler when her father either stepped down or died. She suspected the latter, as he was almost always off fighting in the war in Rasnia or here at the castle recovering from his wounds. It was honestly a miracle she hadn't ended up a child king already, but she was glad for it all the same.

A *king* couldn't fantasize about running away and starting a new life, while an heir still studying the craft could do that all she wanted, even if Nadia knew it wasn't really an option. In all honesty, being able to help their kingdom thrive and recover from her father's war sounded wonderful - the only issue was the fact that those deeds would be connected to the title of 'King' and a name that didn't feel right when she said it.

"You've been staring blankly at me for three paragraphs of script," Jasper announced, and his voice broke her from the thoughts. "Which means I have something on my face, or you're all lost in thought again. You'd tell me if I had something on my face, right?"

"Sorry," Nadia sat back, rubbing her eyes and probably getting charcoal dust on her face. "You look fine, Jasper- I was just… thinking."

"I knew it," Jasper grinned. "I should start placing bets on it."

"Nobody would bet against you when it came to me," Nadia

pointed out. Jasper shrugged, looking back down at the scrolls in front of him.

Transcribing old scrolls didn't usually fall to him, but the youngest apprentices had been ill in the past week, and someone had to do it, so it had been shunted into his workload. He never really complained - Nadia wouldn't be surprised if he was ahead on his work anyway. She would also offer to help, but he was never slow to inform her of the 'atrocious' state her penmanship was. It honestly wasn't *that* bad, he was just a perfectionist.

"So what were you thinking about, Prince?" He asked, dipping his quill in the ink before starting another line, eyes darting between the faded paper and his new one.

Nadia's stomach turned sour at being called that, but she tried her best to ignore the nausea.

"Not much," she sighed. "Just things."

"What things?" Jasper asked stubbornly. Well, Nadia wasn't sure if it was stubbornness or pure curiosity or both, but he wasn't one to let things go.

"History," she said. That wasn't *quite* a lie after all. He smiled at it, though, glancing up for a moment as he continued his work.

"Which history? Or, let me guess - royals who died hundreds of years ago and will never actually affect your life?"

"You're a genius," Nadia said blandly, rolling her eyes. "When have I been lost in thought about any other history?"

"Almost never, that's how I knew."

"Yes, well, I was thinking about how much I wished there were better records of Queen Nadia. You haven't found any mentions in those ones, have you?"

"None that you haven't read before," Jasper set his quill aside, leaning back to stretch his spine against the wooden chair back. Free from the fear of smearing ink, his hands tapped the top of the table a few times as they usually did when they weren't busy. Jasper's hands were almost always busy. "You've probably read everything there is to read about her, Lewis."

"I know," Nadia frowned. *This* is why she shouldn't have thought so much about herself and the fact she was trapped with a name that wasn't hers. Because now, even when her closest friend used it, it made her skin seem to sit on her body inexplicably *wrong*. Like a boot that was two sizes too small and made her foot cramp, but every measurement and every cobbler said it was a perfect fit.

"If I knew how to find more on her, I'd do it in a heartbeat," Jasper said, blinking across at her as his fingers tapped. "But I'm not sure *what* we'd do, aside from raising the dead."

"Well, just do that then," Nadia chuckled. "Easy, raise the dead."

"Magic *is* against the law," Jasper said thoughtfully, tilting his head back to look at the ceiling. "But I'm sure if the old King Arthur hadn't banned it, there would be records of ways to do that. As of right now, I can't. Wouldn't have a clue how to do it, so-"

"I know, J, I was joking." Not only was magic illegal, but most of her teachers seemed to think it was fully extinct. It *was* like Jasper, really, to take such a thing seriously.

"Ah." He smiled, brushing his hair out of his face as he reached to pick up the quill again. "Well, then you know there's nothing we can do. Why don't you research some other ruler - or look more at economics, you struggle with that don't you?"

"Yes, which is why I don't want to study it during my free time."

She really should, though, focus on something useful instead of drawing and losing herself in her own mind like this. She wanted to rule well, and every day she put off her important learning was another day she could get news that King Richard had died, and she was the king. Putting it off was the only way she had to imagine that, maybe, there was a future that didn't make her feel so out of place.

"It'll come in handy when you're king," he quoted blankly - it was what Nadia's tutors always tried to press, reminding her every day of it when she struggled to grasp some concept or another.

"When I'm king, I'll have you to help with that." Nadia shrugged. "And a room full of other advisors who'll want to get their own say on it, anyway."

"I'm a scribe and a scholar," Jasper shook his head. "Not an advisor."

"You can advise me on economics." Nadia knew he was right - the last thing she wanted was to leave herself open to a coup or even a single advisor who wanted to push his own agendas rather than hers, but that problem seemed so far away.

"Okay, well, I'm advising you to study them."

"You're no fun at all, Jasper." Nadia sighed, but got up to cross to the ledgers and trading records from the different territories. He was right, as much as she hated to admit it sometimes.

"I know," Jasper paused, squinting down at the faded page. "You tell me that a lot, I haven't forgotten."

"You never forget anything," it wouldn't really help her case, but she said it anyway. Jasper, in the way he so often did, just nodded.

"Exactly."

Nadia rolled her eyes but spent the next few hours sitting across from him and trying to retain anything at all from the notes on trade and the value of grains from the farms surrounding the capital. It was dull, but it was something to do, and every now and then Jasper would alleviate her boredom with something interesting he'd found in his own work.

* * *

"Prince Lewis, your dinner has been moved to the dining hall for the evening." The news was a surprise, coming from one of the various nursemaids - Julianne - who had been kept on staff to see to Nadia's well-being while her father was off at war.

"The dining hall?" She glanced at Jasper, who just shrugged as he started packing away his scrolls. She hardly ever ate in the dining hall - it was big, and formal, and terribly empty whenever her father was away with the generals at the war front.

"The King wishes to eat with you," Julianne explained, stopping that thought in its tracks. "He arrived back at the castle a few hours ago."

"*Oh-*" she hadn't expected him back yet, unless of course he'd been injured in battle. "Is he alright? Does he- does he actually want to see me, did he *say* that?"

"I haven't seen him," Julianne smiled apologetically. "I'm sure you'll find out soon enough."

"I'll see you tomorrow," Nadia sighed, getting up and smiling at Jasper. He just nodded again, brow furrowed as his fingers tapped along a scroll case. Out into the corridor with Julianne, who fell into step behind her.

Technically, Nadia wasn't ever supposed to just wander through the halls on her own seeing as she was the crown prince, and the only heir to Cidon. Usually, though, Julianne accepted that she would slip away to study with Jasper or sit on the windowsill of her room to read. There was usually some kind of maid or guard around, anyway, so it wasn't like she was *alone*. But when her father was around, the official escort had to be maintained.

Lovely.

"Do you think I look presentable, Julianne?" Nadia paused by a window, frowning at the way her hair had become disheveled, and how there were small ink stains on her hands even though Jasper had been the only one using a quill - she *always* got some kind of transfer from him. "I..."

"You look fine, Prince," Julianne said softly. "They say he's not in a terrible mood, given the circumstances."

That wasn't really anything positive, but at least she seemed to have a *chance* of not being yelled at. It was awful enough to have King Richard lose his temper at her, let alone the audience of butlers and maids that always kept their eyes politely away and their mouths shut afterward. Even Julianne, who used to comfort Nadia back when Richard's yelling still made her cry, never really addressed it aloud. Their silence didn't make Nadia feel any less embarrassed.

So, Nadia made her way through the halls toward the lower levels, where the kitchens and dining hall sat nestled behind the main throne room. Hopefully, Richard wasn't injured again already - he'd only left the castle a few months ago, after recovering from a nasty stab wound to his thigh.

This war had been going on for as long as Nadia could remember. It started when she was young, maybe three or four years old, and hadn't ended in nearly two decades now. She could still remember, though, overhearing as her father received the news of an attack on Rasnia, the kingdom north of Cidon. At the start, they'd just sent supplies and some men, but after the war got worse, and *bloodier*, hundreds of soldiers from Cidon had been sent north on ships or by land to help them.

That was the alliance of Ardenia, after all, that they were to support the other two kingdoms in a time of war. Richard was... incredibly invested, nowadays, enough that he'd started joining the generals and soldiers in Rasnia when Nadia was just becoming a teenager, and was hardly ever home in Cidon since then. The war had dragged on and on for decades, but there had been no talk of peace in a long time.

The king didn't let her into meetings, let alone out in combat, seeing as *Prince Lewis* was his only son and therefore the sole heir. She *was* training in the way of the sword at least - though she wasn't very good at it. Richard was always quick to mention that, and quick to frown whenever he oversaw a training session.

Pushing open the door to the dining hall, she could already smell the talents of the kitchen staff, and it made her stomach rumble. The king was already there, seeming uninjured and already halfway through his food, at the head of the table next to the two empty chairs reserved for Nadia and Queen Anne - whose chair had been empty for Nadia's entire life.

"Ah, Lewis! I was wondering what you'd gotten up to." King Richard was a loud man, and jovial until the imminent moment when *Lewis* didn't live up to his standards. "Where have you been all day?"

"I've been in the library," she said honestly. It's where she usually went, when not in lessons. "Studying with Jasper." She couldn't mention the drawing- even if it was meant to help her precision with a sword, he still saw it as childish.

"Jasper." The king nodded. "Who is that, again?"

"One of the royal scholars," Nadia said for what must have been the hundredth time. "A good friend of mine, he's been helping me study when I'm not in regular lessons."

"Is that all you've been doing with your free time, these days? Not extra *training*?" He frowned over a mug of ale, and Nadia smiled wearily. "You need all the training you can get, from what I hear from Sir Matthew."

This was unsurprising. Both because Nadia had heard it countless times before, and because King Richard was known for his skill in battle - fighting and strategy, but mostly his strength and ruthlessness.

"I've been studying history, mostly." Nadia cleared her throat, picking idly at the plate of food placed before her by a servant. "Past monarchs, and all that. Learning from- from the past, you know?"

"Mm, I suppose. Best to learn from their mistakes, before making your own. But then, of course, it's best not to make any mistakes at all, isn't it?"

"That's what they say," Nadia nodded. "How- how are you? I didn't know you'd be back so soon." He didn't *seem* injured, which was a relief as much as a surprise.

"I'll be here until spring," he sighed. "We've reached a stay of combat, there's already winter storms over the oceans and a temporary treaty was the only reasonable option."

Nadia couldn't help but wonder why they couldn't just come to a permanent agreement - but the war had been going on for years, so it made sense he wouldn't end it now. He never really talked to her about the war. He wanted her more skilled before doing that, which was fair.

Yet, she was nearing the age of eligibility for taking the throne. It wouldn't pass over until Richard died - stars forbid - but... surely at some point, she'd need to know what occurred in those meetings, and on the battlefield.

"Sir Matthew's been saying your swordsmanship is lacking, so you'll have some extra training with him alongside your regular studies starting tomorrow morning." The king continued between bites of food, and Nadia stifled a sigh.

Swordsmanship was one of her least favorite training, though it was her father's most valued skill. With the way the war was going, that made sense. Still, she wasn't fond of it for a few reasons.

The first was that it was *painful*. Sir Matthew was the most talented swordsman in Cidon, after the king, and he wasn't prone to holding back even in a training match. So she usually walked away from it aching and bruised, but that was all supposedly part of the process.

The second was that no women were permitted to learn, so it always felt off and strange to be among the barracks for training even if nobody saw her as a woman except herself. It was silly to care so much about rules that didn't apply to her in anyone else's eyes, but she couldn't help it. Everything was always so uncomfortable, *especially* things that were exclusive to men.

The third and final was that Nadia was far more interested in improving the kingdom from within, rather than fighting other countries. She wasn't sure what she could even do to change the war and whenever she tried to ask anything about it, her father just gave vague answers and changed the subject.

It was starting to get frustrating. Even if nobody knew her as herself, 'Prince Lewis' was only a year and a half from reaching the official age of eligibility to take the throne. Shouldn't the heir know what was going on, even if the current king was healthy?

"You really should try harder," Richard said now, looking at her critically. "Spend less time in those books, more with the guard and with Matthew."

"I enjoy reading," Nadia protested despite herself. She knew the conversation wouldn't get anywhere, but surely Richard could see *some* merit in studying. "Do you really expect the war to be going on by the time I take the throne?"

"For your sake, I hope not." He huffed, impatient. "You wouldn't last a minute in battle, as you are now. You're too nervous, too weak. Honestly, it's as if I was cursed with a daughter instead of a son. All the stars know we'd be doomed if your mother failed me that way as well. It's probably her fault already that you're like this, you know."

"I know," Nadia dropped her head. "My apologies, father."

It hadn't *always* been like this. There were some memories, in the back of her mind, of Richard being closer and genuine. But that was before the war, and before he'd fully come to terms with Queen Anne's death. At some point that had changed, and King Richard had been the rough, abrasive person she was speaking to now ever since.

The only thing Nadia had ever really done right according to him was being born as a boy, instead of a girl, and she could hardly even stomach thinking of herself in that way.

She really shouldn't entertain herself with this name, and changing her thoughts about herself, because none of it would ever become reality. If she had to be uncomfortable in her real life... didn't she at least deserve something for herself? Maybe that was a selfish thought, unfitting for a future king to have.

"I *suspect* the war will end by next autumn either way," he said unexpectedly, going back to eating his food. "If we don't prevail, a marriage treaty for you could end the conflict."

Oh, *great*, just what Nadia needed. Some foreign princess who would expect her to be someone she wasn't, someone she never wanted to be. While she wasn't of age to take the throne, she'd passed the age of legal marriage two years prior, so if her father wanted to marry her off - or, more accurately, marry an Ochean noblewoman or princess into the castle - he could do so at any time.

Nadia wasn't sure if she ever wanted to marry, at least not as Prince Lewis. She'd want to do it as Nadia - *as herself* - if at all.

That wasn't exactly an option. Nausea swirled up from where she usually kept it tamped down, and every part of Nadia's body seemed to wriggle uncomfortably under her skin. *It was just- wrong. She was wrong.*

"I don't have much of an appetite," Nadia said softly, getting to her feet. "I-I may sleep early, to wake up for training with Sir Matthew."

"Alright," King Richard grumbled a bit, roughly putting a hand on her shoulder. "You know I only want what's best for the kingdom."

"I know."

"You must want the same if you plan to take my place one day." He met her eyes, dark brown to the point of being almost black, sitting heavily under his thick brows.

"I know," she said again, smiling weakly. "I'll do my best, I'll do better."

"Good." He nodded, turning back to his food and ale. "I'll watch your training tomorrow, then. Don't disappoint me."

She just nodded, leaving him to his dinner as she went up toward her chambers followed at a short distance by Julianne, who thankfully didn't give any of her usual reassurances. Nadia didn't know if she could get any more words out, tonight, even if it was to someone who meant well.

She was left alone, though, when she reached the inner hallways of the center tower. Of the three towers in the castle here, it was the easiest to defend - and so that's where the royal family slept. The other two held rooms for the staff, and storerooms in the basements, but the center of the castle is where the royal family was safest.

Not that there was much of a *family*, just the two of them until either Richard remarried or Nadia married for the first time. Until today, Nadia honestly hadn't worried too much about getting married- at least not anytime *soon*.

The Rasnians in the north had no eligible heirs - either too young or already wed, but it was incredibly unlikely that Richard would take another wife, after two decades of putting his effort into war instead of anything else, so it seemed that he intended Nadia - or rather 'Prince Lewis' - to take one soon instead which was the very last thing she needed, on top of everything else to make her feel out of place.

If it was to end the war and the king ordered it, there wasn't much she'd be able to do against it. Nadia shut herself into her room, letting the posture she usually held in her back and shoulders drop.

The sun hadn't quite set yet, shining through the western window with rays that reached across the room, bathing everything Nadia owned in reds and oranges. She stepped into one ray, though unlike most days the warmth did little to lift her mood. The mirror against one wall seemed to taunt her, reflecting back the face of a prince - a station that could be proven to anyone in Ardenia by the intricate symbol tattooed on her forearm, marking her forever as the heir to the throne and the future king of Cidon.

Even before the Dolloway family had taken the throne generations ago, they'd had the practice of marking the eldest son like that, and it was *supposed* to be some kind of incredible honor to be able to wear it, but all it did right now was shove Nadia's discomfort and the weight of her future back in her face. She only looked at it for a moment before pulling her sleeve back down, then stepping back to look at herself as a whole.

As far as looks went, Nadia knew she wasn't *unattractive*, but she didn't look like a woman - with stubble along her jaw, and her hair pulled up in a style that only royal men would wear. At least as a royal, she *could* grow it long, and pull it down when she was alone.

That's what she did now, reaching up to tug the pins and cloth keeping it up, letting it fall down around her shoulders. It was a relief - having hair pulled up like that tugged on it, and made her scalp painful and numb after a few hours.

Pulling her hair down still didn't help much, and she turned away from the large mirror before it made her feel any worse. Boots pulled off, left by the wardrobe on one side of the room, and she made her way over to the window to look out, squinting against the sun streaming in.

In the west, past where she could see from the castle, there was the ocean. She'd been there once or twice when she was much younger before the king grew to hate her and before the war had taken over their lives, and the water had gone out as far as the sky. Between there and here, there were miles and miles of farmland and small patches of forest. If she closed her eyes, Nadia could imagine flying over the land and looking down at all the people below.

Farmers, bakers, blacksmiths - peasant children, wooden and stone houses along cobbled streets and dirt roads. She'd never really been to most towns, either staying safe in the castle or in one of the large homes in the cities when she went on a trip with King Richard which wasn't often at all, especially recently.

What was it like, living a normal life with most people not *really* caring what you were - a man or a woman? It had to be less stressful than this, right? Of course, Nadia couldn't know for certain if it was any better than this. She knew she had nicer *things* here, and the best of everything she was given, but that didn't do much to curb the unrest that sat in her chest every waking moment.

How selfish was she, wanting more when she'd been born and raised into royalty?

2

Swords and Soldiers

"Try harder," Matthew's words dug into her chest, and Nadia held back an irritated huff. She was *trying*. It's not like she wanted to be this miserable at everything she ever did, but it's not like he was giving many pointers.

After the first few lessons of different tactics, *years ago*, he'd just been having her spar with him whenever they had lessons… it never resulted in much, aside from dozens of bruises and abrasions when she inevitably failed. He'd even broken her nose once, but since then he'd at least been a bit more careful around her head and face.

Was this really how all the soldiers fighting in the war were taught? How had Rasnia *and* Cidon not been taken by the Ocheans already? It must work for them, somehow, because even after decades of war Cidon still stood strongly to defend their allies.

"In the spring, when combat begins again, do you really want to stay here in the castle and be a coward?" Matthew asked, eyes narrowed as he adjusted his own grip on the practice sword. "Again, and do better this time."

Nadia just nodded, blinking sand out of her eyes as she braced herself for his advance. She wasn't horrible at holding him off, at blocking *almost* every attack, but getting her own into the equation was impossible.

This was useless - Nadia was scrawny compared to Matthew and just about every other soldier she'd met including her father.

If Queen Anne was alive, Nadia suspected she'd look more like her than Richard, despite not being born a girl. Maybe that was just wishful thinking, though, and either way, she'd be cursed to look *wrong*.

Matthew was displeased, and Nadia could only imagine how irritated Richard would be from where he stood on the balcony and watched their training session.

Fighting like she was, a soldier might *survive* a battle. That didn't mean they would win it, or survive the later complications that would come from the wounds. The only reason *she'd* lived this long, even just in training, is that they practiced with dull wooden blades instead of real ones.

The only problem was that Nadia had no idea what she was doing wrong, or how to fix it, and Matthew never offered up any ways to try and fix her mistakes. Simply saying to 'do better' and nothing more. Matthew really didn't need to tell her she was doing it wrong - the bruises on her arms and chest proved that well enough after every training session she'd ever had.

Then she missed a strike, and the point of his blade jammed into her sternum, knocking the wind out of Nadia's lungs in one quick motion. She stumbled back, gasping for breath, and a disappointed sigh came from both in front of her and above her.

"You need to focus," Matthew said with a scoff. "You're too *distracted*, Prince. Get out of your daydreams and focus on the field! Now-"

Whatever he was about to say - unlikely to be helpful to her - was cut off by the sound of a horn that made him turn, looking towards the gates. King Richard sighed again from his place above, and Nadia recovered her breath as the horn sounded again.

"Training is over." Matthew huffed. "I need to greet the wounded men - but be back here *tomorrow*, Lewis."

"Yes sir," Nadia rasped, rubbing her chest as she backed out of the sand pit, while he stalked off in the opposite direction.

That had gone just as terribly as she expected.

Nadia left her practice sword in the rack and shook the sand out of her clothes before going inside, relieved to be out of the sun and the chilly air of the autumn. At least now she had time to go to the library before her other lessons - and maybe her tutors would be busy with the wounded as well, and she could have a bit of a day off. That really depended on how many men were returning, and if the healers needed extra hands, but she could hope for it at least.

The library was mostly empty today - a scribe and a few apprentices on one side of the room, with Jasper on the other. By the same window as always, though this time he wasn't in his chair. He was leaning on the cold brick of the windowsill, squinting down into the courtyard where Nadia had been only a few minutes ago.

"Morning," Nadia dropped into the chair she usually did, raising an eyebrow when he didn't acknowledge her. His fingers were tapping restlessly on the windowsill. "Jasper? *Hello?*"

"Oh- Lewis!" He turned in surprise, cheeks an uncharacteristic pink color when he realized he'd been caught... doing whatever he was doing. What *was* he doing? "I didn't see you, I-"

"It's fine," Nadia rolled her eyes. "What were you looking at?"

"The- well," he sat down, folding his hands together when he usually did if he was trying not to fidget. Why he did this now, Nadia couldn't imagine, because she'd told him countless times that it didn't bother her. "The horn means that the soldiers were returning. Right?"

"Yeah, at least some of them." Nadia shrugged. "Matthew said he needed to greet the wounded, so I'm not sure who all is..."

If Jasper's face had been pink before, it was pale and colorless now. Even his folded hands on the table between them still twisted anxiously.

"Waiting for someone?" Nadia guessed, intrigued. She didn't know Jasper had many other friends - though he had to have *some*, as she wasn't around all the time. He mentioned childhood friends sometimes, and he had more freedom to be social than she did even if he didn't usually take advantage of that. Beyond that, she'd never seen him so anxious. It was unnerving.

"Well- okay," Jasper glanced to the side - but the other scholar and his apprentices seemed oblivious. "I- yeah, one of the- the soldiers is uh- a good friend of mine. And I'm worried about him, but they said this morning there's a winter treaty and I... he's meant to be back soon."

"Oh," Nadia felt like he was keeping some kind of secret, as it wasn't like Jasper to be vague, but figured that was his own business. She had a big secret of her own, didn't she? "When did he go out?"

"A few months ago, in the spring," Jasper said softly, abandoning his attempt to not fidget, reaching to re-arrange his quills and scroll on the desk. "Only a few months! He couldn't have- he wouldn't be actually hurt or killed by now, would he?" It wasn't every day that Jasper said something so clearly untrue to comfort himself. He was actually *worried*.

"Hey," Nadia gently kicked him under the table. "I'm sure it'll be okay. If he's hurt, he has all winter to recover. Right?" Jasper was always luckier than her- if he cared about this person, they were probably alright.

"Well yeah," he didn't seem very comforted. "But I still don't want him hurt. It's like- I mean, when you end up going to fight I'd hate to see you hurt or dead."

"That's sweet," Nadia murmured, while the bruise slowly forming on her sternum throbbed. "But we're at war. Injuries will happen, y'know? That's just how it is."

"I know." Jasper sighed, rubbing his face. "I'm being silly, I know, I just can't focus until I know he's alright."

"I don't think it's silly," Nadia mused, "If you were in battle, I'd be just as worried." Though he never really showed worry like this before, unless an ink bottle spilled on notes or something similar. That's just the kind of person he was, Jasper didn't usually worry much about *people*.

"I'm a scholar, I don't fight," Jasper said. "But I appreciate the sentiment."

He was silent for another few moments, looking back at the window while his paper and quill sat untouched.

"Alright," Nadia sighed and stood. "Come on, we can go greet them."

"What?"

"I'm the *prince*-" The word felt so wrong on her tongue and she grimaced, and Jasper's eyebrows furrowed a bit. Oh, she *needed* to watch herself more carefully. "I should check on the wounded like my father is. And you can come because you're with me."

"Alright," he was on his feet in a moment, tucking in his shirt as he followed her out into the corridors. Huh. Usually, he'd ask more follow-up questions- this was *important* to him. All the more reason to find whoever this soldier was and make sure he was healthy.

It wasn't too long back to the courtyard - transformed from the battle training arena of this morning into a reception of nearly two hundred soldiers. Jasper was fidgeting beside her, tapping his fingers on the sides of his legs with the lack of any table or wall.

Nadia could see the hulking form of King Richard across the way - near a collection of cots where soldiers lay unconscious or near to it. She steered Jasper away from there, glancing at him as he looked around at the men who were milling about and talking to each other.

There were groups of soldiers everywhere, most of whom had a bandage of some kind on their arms, chest, or legs. Some were unconscious on the cots across the courtyard, some were sitting down, or held up by others who weren't as injured. It was a side of the war she wondered if they knew about when they became soldiers, or if they were sold by stories of glory and honor without another thought. None of them seemed disgruntled, though- most of them honestly seemed jovial, and relieved to be home. Even some of the injured soldiers were talking and joking with their friends, or quietly listening to the ones who were, or tending to each other's smaller wounds.

With every five seconds that passed, Nadia could all but feel the dread building in Jasper's chest. He got more fidgety than she'd ever seen him, which was saying something, and his head turned every few seconds, scanning the crowd for whoever this was. She was starting to get frantic too, just seeing him like that, but Nadia tried to swallow that down for Jasper's sake.

"I don't see him," Jasper muttered softly, shoulders collapsing in on themselves. "What if- Lewis, *what if... No,* there's no way he actually got himself hurt."

She didn't know this soldier, but if Jasper cared about him... she wanted him to be okay, too. It *was* strange that she hadn't heard of his soldier friend before, as he usually mentioned his fellow scholars if it came up, but maybe there just hadn't been a good opportunity to talk about him. Or maybe he'd been too afraid that the friend would never return, the way he was clearly thinking now. Or maybe, Nadia had been a bad friend and forgotten it. She hoped it wasn't that one.

"He might not even be in this battalion," she started to say to him. "Just-"

"Jasper!"

An unfamiliar voice burst through the chatter, and Nadia turned to see Jasper being pulled into the arms of a burly foot soldier, still wearing chainmail with a blood-stained bandage around his upper arm, but a wide grin breaking his face in half.

"What are you doing down here?" He asked after a moment, laughing as he let Jasper go. Jasper seemed embarrassed, face bright red as he smoothed his shirt again. "We just got here, how-" The soldier's eyes drifted over Jasper's shoulder to

Nadia, and then widened.

"Lewis," Jasper smiled sheepishly. "This is Ezekiel, the one I told you about."

"Prince, I- I apologize," Ezekiel shifted on his feet. "I didn't know you were here, I uh-"

"No need," Nadia waved a hand. "Any friend of Jasper is a friend of mine, I'm glad you're alright." Of course- a soldier willing to die for the kingdom wouldn't be as casual with her as Jasper always was.

"I'm perfectly fine, I told you not to worry," Ezekiel said, smiling as Jasper looked him up and down.

"You're hurt," Jasper acknowledged, gesturing to the bandage. "What do you need? I can-"

"Oh, that's nothing. Wasn't even combat," Ezekiel laughed. "A tree fell on the road coming back, I helped move it and a branch caught me by surprise. I'm fine, Jasper, I promise."

Nadia knew she was not the smartest person in the world - but she'd been learning for ages how to spot lies and traitors. Ezekiel was most likely not a traitor because that word was a bit dramatic in almost every circumstance, but he was certainly lying about how he'd gotten injured. He shifted on his feet when he said it, and he'd looked above Jasper's head, which was a far cry from the way he'd been looking at Jasper before - which had been the way she imagined a starving man might look at a basket full of food.

She didn't say that out loud, though, instead just watching Jasper curiously. They seemed to be far closer than she'd expected - just how good a *friend* was Ezekiel? And why wouldn't Jasper have mentioned him?

"Alright," Jasper agreed, and *maybe* he knew it was a lie too, but nobody called it out. His shoulders were still tight, posture pulled up past where it usually was when he hunched over books and scrolls all day. "Good. Stay that way, or else."

"Yeah, alright, whatever you say." Ezekiel smiled, patting his chest. "I'm all in one piece, look, I'm unkillable."

"I'll pretend that's even possible, for now," Jasper said with a frown. "But don't think this is over."

"It's sweet you were worried," Ezekiel said softly, shaking his head. "I've got to stay here, check in with Sir Matthew when he calls my line, but I'll find you tonight. Okay?"

"...alright," Jasper nodded reluctantly, glancing at Nadia. "I should head back up- you need to find your father, right?"

"Right," Nadia's heart sank, but she nodded and let Jasper slip away back into a staircase, and when she looked back Ezekiel had melted into the crowd as well. Wonderful. Now she had no excuses at all.

The very last thing Nadia wanted to do was find the king or Matthew, and they *had* dismissed her after training, so she slipped to the side and made her way toward the kitchen entrance. She could just go up to her room from there, Jasper wouldn't expect her back in the library for a while now and she wasn't really in the mood for any lessons or studying.

That and her ribs were still hurting from where Matthew's practice sword had hit them, and she would like to find a place to rest and apply a bruise salve to them without being seen. So, she slipped through the busy kitchen and into one of the back stairways without being noticed. They were probably going to be busy for a while, with the surplus of men suddenly being housed in the barracks when they'd all been away in Rasnia for months - and before that, half of them had lived in town rather than the barracks.

Nadia would probably be able to talk someone into letting

her help out around the castle, doing something or other - Julianne would probably let her carry things between the barracks and the kitchen or laundry room, or fold linens for the injured men if she asked for something to keep her busy.

She was usually told to focus on her studies, but with the stay in combat and a festival coming up, Richard would hopefully be too busy to enforce that and the chaos would make even the most respectful servants want all the help they can get. That and Julianne especially seemed to understand the need for something to do and usually found ways to keep Nadia's hands busy if there was an opportunity.

Today, Nadia was content to shut herself in her room to wait out the initial bustle of the soldier's return. It was still early, and she was usually gone until sunset or even after nightfall, so it did feel a bit strange to be there by herself with the sun still bright overhead.

Avoiding looking at the mirror across the room, Nadia crossed to the shelf above her desk and pulled down a book at random, and the stack of paper she used to draw.

Most books were kept in the library, but she'd either convinced the head scholar to let her take one or smuggled it out when they weren't looking and had collected a few of the duplicate storybooks or historical records she was interested in. Most of the information on the old Queen Nadia was here, and she'd found one record detailing the legend of how she'd taken the throne in the first place.

Jasper had always said that it was hard to trust any history written before King Arthur since he'd been the one to start hiring scribes and scholars into the castle and nobility.

True or not, Nadia had used to imagine that the old Queen and the characters in the stories she read were her friends, who would use a more comfortable name and title for her. It was silly and childish, and it had been a long time since she could distract herself so thoroughly from reality, but it was still comforting to read back through them.

So Nadia settled into a seat by the window, legs drawn up onto it with her, and tried her hardest to let the world fall away in favor of some other one.

She read through pages she already knew as well as herself, then when that didn't help she took a pencil and the papers and tried to draw what she imagined the old Queen had looked like. Then what she wished she would look like, if only she had been born a woman... but she had to put those in the fire, on the off chance that a maid or butler or someone saw them and started asking questions.

Then back to reading, finding storybooks of fairy tales that Julianne had given her as a child to try and lose herself not only in another time, but another world entirely.

It didn't work. Part of Nadia was worried that it would never work again, and she would never escape the discomfort that flowed through every movement, and every time anyone said the prince's name in reference to her.

A more optimistic part figured that another day, when she wasn't as stressed, it would work the same way it had years ago.

Maybe tomorrow. Maybe tomorrow would be better.

She told herself that every single day, but maybe this time it would be true.

3

Fairy Tales

As expected, the castle and the town were both much busier over the next few days. Not that Nadia experienced the chaos of the town herself, but she heard about it from servants and errand boys and she could see the bustling streets even more than usual from the window in her room.

The hectic atmosphere had, as she'd been hoping for, made Matthew cut a few of her training sessions short, and her other tutors were absorbed in their work and more distracted, giving her more time to slip away and find Julianne or another older member of the staff, who she could sway into letting her help with little things. Whether they were just tired of her pestering at this point, or they actually appreciated the help, she wasn't sure and honestly didn't want to know.

Either way, Nadia spent as much time as she could helping to prepare simple parts of meals, helping Julianne move linens to the washrooms, and other odds and ends that she could do to keep herself out of sight and *hopefully* out of her father's attention outside of meals, where she had no real choice but to sit and try to carry on a conversation with him, as difficult as that was.

The library was one place that hadn't changed much with the arrival of the soldiers, all the scholars were still occupied doing their studies and transcriptions. If anything, there were more scholars going in and out as they carried journals recording injuries and deaths up from where they'd been interviewing generals.

It was a good distraction, being able to be doing something at every minute of the day. There was less time to glimpse herself in a mirror or a window's reflection, but there was more time to think about the fact that nobody in the world knew who she really was, except herself. Idle tasks left her mind wandering, and it always came back around to that no matter how much she tried to ignore it.

She was Nadia. She was Prince Lewis. She was Nadia. She was the Future King.

The thing about kings, at least as far as Nadia knew, is that they were expected to be truly *great*. Every king in recent history had made a name for himself, literally or figuratively - or even after their deaths, the people would assign a title beyond 'king' to whoever had led them for years if not decades.

Old King Arthur, of course, was the Defender of Light. The First New King of the age of the Dolloway throne - he'd banned evil magics and he'd brought Cidon back into the good graces of the stars, reuniting Ardenia from what had become fractured in the years before him.

Then there was The Dragon Slayer - Arthur's grandson - who had led quests into the wildlands and mountains to find dragons and slay them and take their hoards back for the people of the land. Even today, in the most protected parts of the castle, there were scaly hides from his exploits preserved and hung on the walls.

Then of course Hugo Dolloway, Nadia's grandfather, was said to have had a close connection with the very gods themselves. He was said to have spoken to the stars nightly and gained a better understanding of the world and all its aspects during his time as the king.

She had never met her grandfather, though, because he had died of some illness and left the throne to Richard, who was still the king to this day. King Richard was still building his legacy, but scholars and bards had already begun to write him in as a Soldier King, a man who wasn't afraid to risk everything for the land that he ruled over.

Then there was Prince Lewis. The heir to the throne, King Richard's only son... and the person that Nadia had to be.

She had no idea what kind of legacy she would be able to leave- half the time it was hard for her to even imagine a future, but she had to. The future was all that mattered.

Maybe her legacy would be an alliance with the Oceans, and future scholars would call her a peacebringer or a uniter of the people. That would be nice, Nadia wouldn't mind that. She wanted to see Cidon thrive, and she wanted to see Rasnia find true peace and she wanted to strengthen their connection to Ashan - and she would be marrying an Ochean princess, it seemed, so putting Ochea on her list of places to connect to only made sense.

Nadia wished she knew more about what had to be done, what could be improved, and what could be lifted up into the stars the way other kings had before her. All of Cidon's focus in recent decades had been on the war, helping Rasnia keep from falling, and keeping the Oceans at bay across the sea and on the coast. Was there infrastructure she could be planning to build upon? Were there temples in disrepair, that she could fix in honor of her grandfather and the gods he'd loved so much?

Was there anything she could do to make Lewis Dolloway stand out in the history of Cidon as much as her ancestors? There were eight generations of expectations, and Nadia didn't know how she'd meet a single one of them.

Nadia frowned, looking down at the mark on her arm that labeled her so clearly as the upcoming leader. Every single king for the past three centuries had worn a tattoo like this all their lives. Even Arthur, who hadn't been born into royalty and who had clawed his way to the top to bring peace, had the Dolloway's symbol inked into his skin.

It was like a curse, almost. It was a promise that Nadia hadn't willingly made but still one she had to keep. If she didn't, Cidon would crumble and take Ardenia down with it, and they'd fall back into a time of chaos and civil wars.

Nadia had been so *young* when they'd put the mark on her arm - all she remembered thinking was that it would match her father. It was so long ago that Richard hadn't turned cold yet, and the world still seemed so bright and uplifting that she'd sat through the pain and the tears and let her small arm be tattooed. Ever since, as well, whenever she grew a bit too much or it faded a bit too pale, Nadia would sit patiently and endure the process once again, but she'd done it a bit more spitefully in recent years.

All the mark did these days was remind her of who she was supposed to be, and the fact that everything about her was wholly inadequate, and she had started to despise Prince Lewis as a concept.

'Prince Lewis' wasn't a bad person to be, and Nadia knew

that. Ever since she'd first tried to understand who she was as a person, she'd known that it just wasn't the *right* person to be for her.

She had to be him, at least when she was around anyone else. That was the only downside to the busyness now. It was becoming exhausting, having far less time alone to let her posture drop and pull her hair down.

Really, Nadia had thought she was doing a good job of hiding the weariness that seemed to ebb away at her very soul.

"You're tired," Jasper said matter of factly, setting down his quill in the middle of- whatever he was doing. Nadia was pretty sure he'd finished transcribing but hadn't felt like asking what his most recent project was.

"What do you mean?" Nadia sat back to get a different angle of the portrait sitting in front of her, all charcoal smudges and lines as she attempted to get Jasper's profile right, and apparently in her focus she'd let her composure drop.

Was she really so obvious that even Jasper could tell? He knew her better than most, but he usually seemed oblivious to things like that. Though she wouldn't put it past him to notice something and *ignore* it if he didn't find it important enough.

"Tired or upset," Jasper amended, eyes narrowed as he studied her. "I can't tell, but you've been either tired or upset for a whi- for the past few days. Are you sick or something?"

The library was full and bustling with the sounds of quills and charcoal pencils on paper, but they were tucked away in the corner they usually sat in and nobody seemed to be paying them any attention.

"I'm alright," Nadia waved it off anyway, leaning back to stretch.

"So you're upset, then," Jasper nodded thoughtfully. "What

are you upset about?"

"I'm not upset! If anything, you were right about me being tired." Nadia shook her head. What did Jasper even know? *Nothing*, he was just... the smartest person she knew, that's all. "But I'm fine, really, it's just been... busy."

"It has been a lot recently," Jasper agreed. "It'll calm down in a few weeks, though, once winter sets in. Then it'll be a few months before all the soldiers leave again, back to Rasnia."

"If they even do," Nadia muttered, a strange twist in her stomach as she thought about what her father had said. Being married seemed, if it was possible, even less exciting now than it had when he first mentioned it.

"What do you mean? Why wouldn't they?"

"Well-" Nadia winced, glancing around to make sure they were still being ignored, and they were. Still, she lowered her voice and leaned forward so only Jasper had any chance of hearing her. "My father said they might come to an agreement, maybe a... marriage treaty. Or something."

"Is that why you're upset?" Jasper guessed, fingers beginning their usual rhythm upon the table. "Because you might be married soon?"

"I- I don't know," Nadia sighed. That was just one string in the complicated knot her emotions were in. It's not like that was something she could really discuss with anyone - *Jasper* just wasn't one for emotions, and the *king* found emotions a weakness. "I just don't like thinking about it."

"That won't stop it from happening, if the Ocheans agree."

"I know *that*, I just..."

"I understand it's probably an unpleasant concept," Jasper said thoughtfully. "Most people would want to marry someone they know. You've never met any of the Ocheans, we've been at war with them for most of your life. But the fact is that no matter what, *your* marriage will probably end up being political rather than the result of a relationship. You're the prince, you'll be king once your father dies- stars forbid it."

"I know," Nadia felt sicker at his words, though he obviously didn't mean any harm. She didn't want to be reminded that she was a prince, and a man, and would never be what she wanted to be.

"I upset you," Jasper said then, sitting back. "What did I say that upset you? I- I don't *actually* think the king will die anytime soon."

"It's nothing," Nadia rolled her eyes. How could Jasper be so oblivious to some things, but still know the very *moment* she was upset? Just another bit of evidence that he wasn't oblivious at all, and just ignored how other people felt most of the time. Nadia wasn't sure which one would be funnier. "You didn't upset me, Jasper. You could never upset me, and you're right."

"So you *are* upset because of the marriage treaty?"

"Well-" and that was just it, wasn't it? Nadia wasn't against the idea completely - except for the words associated with it. "No. I mean- not really. It's not perfect, but I could deal with it."

"So what's wrong?" Jasper sighed, shaking his head. "I'm your friend and I want to help, but I don't know what's going on with you."

"I..." Nadia hesitated, looking down at the drawing of Jasper instead of the real one sitting across from her.

What was she doing? She could never tell anyone about this- she knew that. But Jasper, her best friend in the world, was sitting there staring at her with those stupid wide eyes of his. He was one of the kindest people she knew, and he was just asking her to be *honest* with him.

"I want the war to end." She said softly. "If that means I marry a stranger, so be it. I also know that when my father dies, I'll become the ruler of Cidon. But I can't stand the thought of being a husband, or being a king."

"What do you mean?" Jasper asked. "What else would you be?"

"Well... a queen."

The table between them was silent for a moment, and Nadia was suddenly nauseous again, realizing just how many people could have overheard that. It was bad enough she'd said it to Jasper... Oh, stars- he was going to say she was crazy.

He was going to say she was crazy, and then he'd never want to talk to her again, and Nadia would be alone in this world with not even Jasper's rambling explanations to distract her from herself. What was she thinking? She couldn't say this- she couldn't tell *anyone* about this! Everyone here was going to look at her the same way her father did, and then what?

After a few seconds too long, she forced herself to look up at Jasper. He didn't *seem* upset... or even confused. Instead was sitting back whispering something under his breath, pushing his hair back out of his eyes.

"You want to be a queen." He finally repeated, as quietly as he'd ever been, looking back at her.

"Yeah." Oh, what had Nadia *done*? She was stuck in this now, trapped in however Jasper was going to react. She only hoped he wouldn't say what he really thought to her face, Nadia didn't know if she could take that.

"And if you weren't the heir, what would you want to be?" He asked curiously. "A peasant woman? Or a-" Oh, she wished he wasn't asking follow-up questions right now. Nobody had even looked their way, both of their voices getting lost and dampened in the papers and books and bustling of the room, but she still...

"Yes," Nadia nodded, stomach turning over itself as she tried to find a way to fix her mistake. Maybe if she could just *explain* it to him, then... "I know it's not... It's a ridiculous thing to want. But I can't help it. Thinking about myself like a- a prince, or the king... a *man* it just feels wrong, I feel sick or something, I don't know how to explain it."

"So it's not about being married or being the heir at all," Jasper summed up. "Just about being seen as a man."

"...yeah." Nadia didn't know what she'd expected, but Jasper was so much calmer about this than she'd expected. He was acting like this was just... *normal*. Where was the judgment? Where was the confusion, and him saying she was crazy and talking about the star's will and her role as the prince and... and where was any of what she'd expected?

"Okay," Jasper hummed thoughtfully. "And your name, Lewis, do you want that to be something else too?" Was he actually... alright with this?

"Nadia." She said softly - it felt so strange to finally say it out loud. "I-I want my name to be Nadia."

"Nadia," came the parroted reply, then a scoff. "I should've known that. You're always looking for information on her."

"I mean- I find her interesting," Nadia said numbly, still reeling. "And I thought who better to take the name of than another queen?"

"It suits you," Jasper said. *What?* "How long have you felt like this?"

"I dunno," Nadia frowned. "Years, forever really... it's gotten worse as time went on. And now with this treaty in the possibilities... I don't know. I've just been thinking about it more and more."

"Sorry if this is a dumb question, but why haven't you told anyone? Like your father... Surely *you* of all people can just be who you want to be?" Jasper- no way. Not only was Jasper not horrified by her, but he actually thought she could tell *other* people? Did they live in the same *world*- let alone *castle*?

"He'd be upset with me," Nadia said. "I don't know why you're taking this so well, actually. I feel crazy, and you're just acting like I'm not, and..."

"You're not crazy, Nadia." Hearing him say her name was jarring, but not exactly in a bad way. She looked across to find his expression deadly serious. "Doesn't this happen all the time? Like that old story of the Ashan nursemaid who became a king?"

"That's a fairy tale." No *way*.

"Well yeah, most of it, but the actual story happened." Jasper blinked at her. "It was a long time ago, but Ashan has always been much better at recording their history. It was their King Tiras, born as a commoner girl, who grew up to be a nursemaid for a noble family *before* disguising himself as a man to join the army and fight against the southern raiders. He then became king for his heroics, and never went back to being a woman. A lot of sources say that it wasn't just to keep the throne, either, because *he* developed the council they have now, with no one throne."

"A lot less dramatic than the storybook," Nadia noted, and couldn't help but smile as he rattled off the obscure facts as if they were common knowledge. He... didn't hate her. He thought this was just- just *fine*. The world hadn't crumbled to dust as soon as she said this out loud.

"Well I was leaving out all the details," Jasper shrugged. "And the fairytale version includes magic helping him present himself that way, and since it's banned now, any accurate records have been erased. At least in our records. I've never been to Ashan, but I've *heard* they're less strict on that... stuff."

"Interesting..." Nadia had known that tale for most of her life, and it had always been told as if it was just a story, nothing more. One of the ones Julianne would tell her, as a very young child, to help her fall asleep at night.

It was one of the first things, honestly, that had put words to how she felt about herself - but it was a children's story, just a tall tale... except Jasper didn't lie or even really joke, and he spent his entire life here reading through history. So she didn't have much choice but to believe him.

"I can get you those records if you want," Jasper added. "And there are others that are similar, though most aren't about royalty or nobles so they aren't written down, just told through word of mouth."

"Really?" Nadia had never thought there were other people who might actually feel this way. That was... *wow*.

"Yeah," Jasper paused thoughtfully. "A good half of them do refer to *some* kind of- of magic... that's probably why you haven't heard them. Nobody would want to talk about illegal magic in front of *royalty*."

"That, and my father is..." Nadia sighed, shaking her head. "The way he is. I don't know what he'd even say if I told him about this, but I know he'd be upset with me." Why wasn't *Jasper* upset with her? Was this actually- was this actually a thing? She wasn't crazy?

"How do you know if you haven't told him?"

It was almost a fair question - Jasper had only ever spoken

to King Richard once or twice in his life, and never one-on-one. He hadn't been there for the hours of berating Nadia had, basically anytime the man was home at the castle. How was she even supposed to explain it? Jasper had a good relationship with his own father, he wouldn't understand.

"You don't have to tell anyone if you don't want to," Jasper said when she didn't answer. "I'm just trying to understand."

"I know you are." If there was one thing she knew about Jasper, it was that he wanted to understand everything there was to understand in the world.

"Thank you for telling me," Jasper said then, hands fidgeting, picking at the wood on the table. "You're my best friend. I *want* to know you."

"You want to know everything." Nadia pointed out, and Jasper grinned.

"Well, yeah, but knowing you is *pretty* high on the list." He paused, leaning back in his chair again to look out the window, then back at her. The library bustled the same way it had been before she told him her secret, and a glance around showed nobody was interested in their conversation in the slightest. "So what are you gonna do?"

4

The Festival

The answer to Jasper's question, at least for now, was a whole lot of nothing. The kingdom was *busy* and the castle was *busy* and Nadia, along with it, was far too *busy*. Everyone was preparing for a cold autumn and winter, and while no snow had fallen yet she could see the tops of the mountains in the distance, white with snow and clouds.

Soon there would be the winter's festival, and once the sun rose the day after that the change of seasons would be officially underway. Then it would be a crowded winter with their cities and barracks full once again, soldiers recovering from wounds and training for the battles in the spring.

Nadia still didn't really understand a stay in combat instead of ending the war, but she'd never really understood war in the first place. She'd always held onto the hope that it would end before she would have to deal with it, and maybe it *would* end, but marrying into a family they'd been fighting for decades was a far cry from 'not having to deal with it'.

That was only one of her many worries, as the days pulled on and grew chillier and into browns and reds and oranges as the harvest pulled in. The only real respite she had were the moments she was alone, and now, the moments she was alone with Jasper. He knew, and he was *okay with it*, and she hadn't expected it to come as such a relief to hear someone else use the right name.

It would feel silly, if it didn't make her so unexpectedly *happy*.

"Nadia," it happened again now, as Jasper strolled up beside her in the corridor, where she'd found a spot by a window where she could sit and watch the decorations being put up in the city, and draw a mimicry of the people and animals down below even though she couldn't see enough details to really do well. "You're going to the festival with Ezekiel and I, tomorrow night."

"What?" She almost laughed at that. "Since when do *you* go to festivals?" It's not that Jasper hated *fun*, but he hated being around a lot of people and noise and that's why she could almost always expect him to be in the library.

"Since Ezekiel wants me to go," Jasper said simply, and squinted out the window as well. "And you *have* to go, being the heir, so would you rather be with us or with your father on that podium all night?"

That was a good point. She had never participated in the festival before- Jasper had never wanted to and she had no other friends. Not to mention it was more 'dangerous' to actually go out into it, but with Ezekiel being a soldier and guard, it would be easier to go around with him than it would be just with Jasper.

"You still could've asked, instead of just telling me." Nadia pointed out, though she knew it probably hadn't been his intention to be rude at all.

"Why would I ask you if I already knew what you were going

to say?"

"You didn't know for certain, you just *assumed.*"

"Okay, *fine*," Jasper rolled his eyes. "Do you know why there are only two *seasonal* festivals, instead of four?"

"Why?" When in doubt, he always went back to history. Nadia didn't mind listening, even though these stories were told to every child in the Kingdom, including herself. Jasper liked to talk, and she liked to hear it even if she'd heard it a million times before. As he did with many things, Jasper was trying to use their shared interest in history to convince her to go with him.

"Thirty-five years ago, give or take, there was a year with no autumn," Jasper explained cheerfully. "The summer was long and hot and dry, and then *all of a sudden* the snow came and it was cold and the land was covered in snow. From the middle of Ashan to the north of Rasnia, it was winter too soon, and had been summer too late."

"So they changed everything about the festivals?" It was an easy prompt, even though she knew Jasper would have kept telling the story anyway.

"The king at the time, your grandfather, fell ill." Jasper continued. "And he declared that they must have angered the god of the sky and the god of the land. Now, your father doesn't do much with religion but that can't be said for the kings before him. The festivals were initially to honor gods, and the usual autumn festival was for the god of Harvest."

"A *minor* god." Nadia agreed, and Jasper smiled.

"Exactly. *So* out of jealousy, the gods of the sky and land took away the possibility of a celebration to someone other than themselves, the main eight gods." Jasper summed up. "The festivals were redesigned, one in the middle of spring to welcome in the summer, with the festival of Birth and Land. Then one in the middle of autumn, to welcome winter with the festival of death and sky. And the next year, the seasons went back to normal."

"And so it's been ever since," Nadia finished for him with a flourish, and Jasper nodded.

"Two seasonal festivals, and other small ones for other things." Jasper agreed. "So you'll go with us? *Please?*"

"Sure," Nadia fought back a grin. "That sounds fun."

"You were going to say that anyway, weren't you?" Jasper scowled at her, and Nadia just laughed. "I don't understand why you're like this." He informed her. "I think you and Ezekiel will get along well."

"And why do you say that?" From the small conversation they'd had, Nadia didn't have much opinion about the soldier. He was clearly enthusiastic, or maybe he was just naturally happy. Whatever he really was, he seemed pleasant enough.

"I don't understand him most of the time either." Jasper frowned, reaching to rap his knuckles against the windowsill before letting his fingers drop to tap there.

"I'll just have to check with my father... would Ezekiel be alright being an escort, or should I get another guard to follow me around?" Nadia sighed, folding her arms. "There's no way I'd be allowed to just... run off with you. Not in town."

"Oh, he'll probably do it. I'll still ask, though." Jasper hummed softly. "Do you think Ezekiel likes history?"

It was a completely random question, and Nadia leaned on the wall, considering it as a banner was raised on the road between the castle and the town.

"You know him better than I do, isn't he a good friend of yours?" She asked curiously. "He wasn't raised as a scholar, so he probably has less access to *learning* history. But he knows you, so he has all the access he really needs."

"Not everyone likes to talk about history all the time," Jasper said it as if it was the worst thing in the world, and to him it just might be. "Sometimes I think I'm boring to him."

"He found you in a crowd of soldiers and yelled your name." Nadia pointed out. "I'd say he likes you enough that he doesn't care if you're boring." There was no way Jasper was *that* oblivious. Surely he knew, surely he'd seen how Ezekiel looked at him.

"Well..." Jasper tapped his fingers along the windowsill. "I suppose that's a good point. He probably wouldn't have stayed m-my friend for so long, if he cared."

He must care more about this 'friendship' than anyone reasonable if Jasper of all people doubted facts he already had. Nadia *had* thought, that day, it was odd how red Jasper's face got when Ezekiel was there. It was just as red now, rising up into his face that was usually so pale from being indoors at almost every time of the day.

...Was this a group of friends going to a festival she was joining, or something else that Ezekial might not be as happy about? Did Jasper even know, if it was, that he might want it to just be the two of them? Hmm. She might have to brace herself for a night as the prince after all, depending on what it seemed like when they got there.

"When did you two become *friends*, anyway?" She asked curiously, and Jasper hummed.

"Three... three years ago. I think. Maybe two and a half."

"What? *Years*? Jasper, how come you've never told me about this before?" Nadia laughed. Jasper usually only did things he thought made sense, so he probably had some oddly practical reason for it.

"You never asked."

And there it was.

"So you think he's been friends with you for two or three years, but he doesn't like you?" She chuckled. "I've never seen you this nervous before."

"Sure you have, you just don't have a good memory."

"That- okay," while true, it was rude to bring up. "I don't think you have anything to worry about."

"Well if you think so," Jasper nodded to himself, and it was odd for him to ask her opinion on much of anything. Not because he didn't care for it, but because as he'd said just minutes ago, anything she thought he probably already knew or agreed with. "I'll uh- oh! I'll see you tomorrow, Prince," and he straightened up, bowing lowly while footsteps echoed at the far end of the corridor. "Have a good night of rest, so you can enjoy the festivities?"

"You too, Jasper."

He didn't need to be so formal, but at least he hadn't let anyone in on her secret. It was only a pair of maids walking down toward the laundry room, arms full of linen that, from the looks of it, had come from the barracks. Unless someone here in the castle had suffered a bad nosebleed.

Jasper's eyes caught onto the blood as well and he frowned, but with his performance of a farewell already done he was walking away. Nadia nodded to the two maids before turning back to the window, thoughtful.

Both Jasper and herself had learned something about the other, recently, despite years of knowing each other best. Nadia of course had known her own secret, and Jasper's had probably been unintentional. Still, it was strange to learn something so new about him after so long.

It had to be the same for him, though, so it was only fair. And now she had something to think about other than herself and her own problems, she could think about just *what* this Ezekiel might mean to her best friend.

* * *

"I'd like to join the festivities tonight, Father," Nadia murmured softly, leaning over toward his chair on the podium after he'd given the usual speech about the end of the year and the grace of the god of the skies. "Will I be missed?"

"About time you did something other than sit and read," he was already a drink or so into the night and didn't seem to care at all. Perfect. "Take a guard with you, and *stay* within the firelight."

"I will," she glanced to the base of the podium, where Ezekiel was waiting next to the on-shift guards for the festival. He bowed his head respectfully when she met his eyes, so at least he didn't seem completely annoyed with her for making him work on his night off.

"Be safe, don't do anything stupid *or* make a mockery of us." Came the final suggestion from the king, before he waved her away.

"Right." she dipped her head and stood, joining Ezekiel on the ground.

"My prince," Ezekiel dipped his head in a bow again, stiff and respectful.

"You can call me whatever you want," Nadia said. "I don't really care." It wasn't true, but if this was someone Jasper cared about she didn't want him to think he needed to be formal in any way.

He just shrugged, then led her to the edge of the crowd where Jasper was waiting.

"Lewis!" Jasper beamed, and as committed as he was to using the right name when they were alone, it was a relief to see he could use the wrong one around this many people. He'd slipped up once or twice in the library before now, but it never seemed to catch anyone's attention. The scholars were probably used to overhearing their conversations about obscure history, and any that might have eavesdropped had given up on it years ago. Tonight, though, Nadia could sense the eyes of townsfolk on her back.

It wasn't often she ever joined into something like this.

"Ezekiel was going to tell me about what Rasnia is like," Jasper said enthusiastically. "You haven't been there either, have you?"

"Unfortunately not," Nadia sighed. "But you know everything there is to know about Rasnia already, don't you? Why would you need to go?"

"Knowing something and experiencing something," Ezekiel spoke up. "Are two very different things, Prince Lewis. Would you like to hear what it is to *experience* a summer in Rasnia, or do you want to rely on books?"

"Tell us, tell us," Jasper insisted. "Let's get some food and you can tell us about it, Ezekiel!"

Nadia raised an eyebrow, finding that Jasper's eyes were alight in a way they only were when he was rambling passionately about something. But instead of that, he was eager to listen to someone else - which was a rare sight indeed.

"Tell us about Rasnia," she agreed. "I haven't been debriefed on the specifics of anything there yet, I'm interested in your thoughts on it."

"Oh, don't be all *princely*." Jasper huffed, and Nadia almost outright smiled at his expression of dramatic disgust. "Lewis likes learning just as much as I do, Ez, sh-he- he's just nervous because he doesn't know you yet."

"Ah, of course." Ezekiel let Jasper pull him through the crowd toward a food stand, and Nadia trailed along as he began his story. "Well, even being north of us it's just as hot in the middle of the day, but it's bitterly cold at night. Less humid, though, you know they have fewer rivers and swamps."

"Oh, that must be nice," Jasper handed Nadia a meat pie, but still seemed wrapped up in only what Ezekiel was saying. "I hate humidity, it makes paper get moldy if you don't store it right."

Hm. She might just be right in her suspicions, but Nadia wanted to get a better read on Ezekiel first. Too bad she was royalty, and he wasn't acting like he probably did around anyone else. It was something to note, but she was sure she could still get some kind of an understanding of him tonight. They passed by a stand of ale and she took one when the soldier did, though she knew well enough now that Jasper didn't like the way it tasted, and sure enough, he didn't take one.

"It also makes wearing armor absolutely miserable, not as much so up there." Ezekiel agreed. "But then without the humidity you might find it dry and itchy, Jasper, there's things to complain about no matter where in the world you go."

"It's even drier in Ashan, isn't it? With their deserts." Jasper found a seat at an old wooden table by the fence, away from the center of the square, and started picking through the meat pie while they joined him.

"We're not fighting any wars in Ashan, so I've never been.

That, we'll have to rely on books for." Ezekiel shrugged, then cleared his throat. "What about you, prince? Where's your favorite place to travel?"

"Oh," Nadia looked up from her pie, almost surprised. They both seemed so focused on each other, she was enjoying being able to just listen. "I don't travel much, I'm afraid. I went to the coast a few times as a child, but I've never left our borders. The king finds it too dangerous for me, seeing as we're at war now."

"Ah, of course." He smiled thinly, as if Nadia had just met some unfortunate expectation. "I know you're not much for the people, Prince, but I do appreciate you joining us tonight."

Now what on earth did *that* mean? It was barbed with something, and she wasn't sure she liked what Ezekiel was implying.

"Who says I'm not for the people?" She protested. "I love the people."

"Do you now?" Ezekiel hesitated, glancing over at Jasper who seemed baffled by their exchange, still chewing on a bite of his own food. "You're friends with Jasper, Prince, I assume that means you're used to people being blunt with you?"

"Hey!" Jasper swallowed quickly, choking on his words. "What's that supposed to mean?"

"It means you say what you mean and nothing else," Nadia chuckled.

"That's called being clear and efficient, not *blunt...*"

"Be blunt with me, Ezekiel," she said, and with the badly hidden smirk he held at the words she figured he'd been wanting to even before she offered it. *Oh, he didn't like her, did he? Oh no.* "Any friend of Jasper's is a friend of mine, I told you that. If you have something to say just say it."

"Everyone knows you're a shut-in," Ezekiel said simply. "And there's nothing *wrong* with that. But we are at war, you know? The king spends his time among the people and the soldiers fighting it, and you do not. You are *not* for the people."

"Oh, be fair at least! Lewis is still training and studying to become a ruler," Jasper said defensively. "He has to stay safe, too, he can't just walk around town like we can."

"I'm not saying it's a bad thing, but it's the truth." Ezekiel shrugged. "And with you being Jasper's friend, it only makes sense you share his habits of staying indoors. But don't claim to know your people if you don't. You did tell me to be blunt, didn't you?"

"I'd be disappointed if you were anything but." Nadia bit the inside of her cheek, thinking over what all he'd just said. She was fairly good at reading people, after years of diplomacy lessons and bored people-watching, but it seemed that he was the same and she hadn't expected that from a simple soldier.

It *was* true. She spent her life sequestered by maids and butlers and was only really in contact with anyone who worked within the castle. It was a secluded life, certainly, but she hadn't really thought much of it until just now. Not really, not beyond fantasizing about a possible other life she could have if she was born elsewhere. Maybe that was even part of the problem, assuming things without going out to see them.

"If there was one thing you'd want me to know of the people, then," she asked slowly. "If I wanted to try and change that, what would you tell me?"

"I'd tell you to look outside yourself." Ezekiel gestured past her, back toward the chattering crowd of the festival, toward the center of the town where people were dancing and music was playing over all the hundreds of conversations. "If you're

THE FESTIVAL

as smart as Jasper says you are, you'll figure out what you need to know on your own. That's what I was saying about experiencing rather than knowing."

"See, I knew you two would get along," Jasper announced, and Nadia couldn't help but laugh. She wasn't sure if Ezekiel liked her at all, but he was definitely well-spoken and easy to talk to, which she knew wasn't very true for herself.

The soldier smiled as well, returning his attention to Jasper now and Nadia took that moment to do exactly what he'd advised, pushing past the overwhelming noise and taking in the festival around them. It was easy to watch and understand one person at a time - but crowds were another thing entirely.

The sun was fully set now, and it was chilly, but most of the people here were wrapped in thick cloaks and jackets as they danced and sang and enjoyed the night together.

It almost reminded her of faint memories of noble celebrations in the ballroom in the castle, but that had been a long, long time ago and she'd only seen it when she snuck out of bed to the balcony to watch. Even back then, before she'd thought much about it, Nadia had wished she could look as beautiful as all the noblewomen in their gowns did.

No grand parties had been hosted in the castle since the start of the war, most nobles being generals or weapon masters who were as busy as the king was these days. *These* were just people, the families of those who'd raised her in her father's stead.

If Nadia had found watching people in town from the windows of the castle interesting, this was even more so. Despite the noise and the crowding, it did give a bit of a different idea of it all. The dances weren't formal ones she'd learned a few years ago, but fast and simple folk kinds she'd watched idly from over a book on other festival days, days when she sat up on the podium with the king until he went home early, separate from the world even when she was supposedly with them.

Jasper had asked her to actually participate a bit today, so here she was with him instead of in the chair beside the king.

Quite suddenly the scholar was on his feet, and Nadia looked over in surprise.

"There- hold on, there's my sister," he stammered, tripping over himself. "I'll be right back!" His sister and parents, who Nadia had only seen once or twice and never really spoken to, were indeed across the square around the bonfire that had started up at sunset. From what she recalled, they were merchants who owned one of the finer textile shops in the city.

Then he was off, ducking through the crowd toward them, and Nadia found herself alone at the table with Ezekiel. He stared after Jasper, looking only a bit disgruntled.

"Is your family here as well, Ezekiel?" She asked. This was a good opportunity to try and get to know more about him when he wasn't distracted by Jasper's presence.

"No. They live around the lake's edge, in Stonewell." He said simply. "I haven't seen them in a good few years now, but their letters say all is well."

"Are you taking a leave for the winter to visit, or are you staying here with the armies in the barracks?" Nadia asked curiously.

"Staying." Ezekiel sighed, turning back toward the way Jasper had gone, and Nadia huffed slightly. "What?"

"Be honest with me one more time," she requested, and he nodded with a grin. "Was this meant to be a night you spent alone with him? I'd really hate to be intruding, but he asked me to come and..."

Ezekiel's smile faded slightly, and he stretched his arms over his head and leaned back with a hum.

"Any time with Jasper is time well spent," he said then. "He wanted you here, and you accepted. Turning away the prince would not bode well for my career or my life."

"You wouldn't be turning me away," Nadia shook her head. "If I happened to have business elsewhere, nobody would know. I'd find another guard to follow me around, and let you have your... time."

"What, and let you get away with sitting back up there and not experiencing anything?" Ezekiel shook his head. "Not a chance, Prince. You're more fun to talk to than I expected. I can spend time with only him later."

"What did you expect, then?" Nadia asked. "You seem to have a lot of expectations for me having only met me once, did I give you that bad of a first impression?"

"You have no *idea* how much the people of this town gossip, and sometimes that topic falls on you, Prince." Ezekiel chuckled. "There's a lot of ideas about you, and why you stay up in that castle all day long. Your first impression proved some of them wrong, and so you're *interesting*. And Jasper likes you, so there must be something about you that's worthwhile."

Worthwhile.

If that's what he was looking for, Nadia couldn't help but think that Ezekiel was going to be very disappointed.

5

Ifs and Buts

The thing about telling Jasper her secret was that now that *someone* knew, Nadia wished everyone could know and just accept it the way he had. That wasn't exactly an option, and there was so much else to focus on and think about that caring about herself and her *situation* felt selfish, especially after spending time with Ezekiel at the festival.

He made good points, about how King Richard did interact more with the people and soldiers of the war than she did. Nadia had never once imagined how the people of the kingdom might see her - or rather, how they saw Prince Lewis. She'd honestly avoided thinking about it because she knew they saw her as exactly that, a prince, and that was too much to think about sometimes.

Apparently, they saw a *shut-in*. Ezekiel hadn't elaborated much on that, once Jasper rejoined them he'd been distracted from the conversation again and Nadia had spent the rest of the night drinking a bit more, and watching and listening to the people around her as best she could.

Prince or Princess, King or Queen, Nadia wanted to be a good *ruler* if nothing else. She at least wanted to try to keep up the reputation of the royal family and make the land a bit happier if she could.

She *was* the only heir, and she had the mark to prove it, and beyond that, Nadia was sure that she could make good changes in the world. Being who she wanted to be had to at least go alongside that, if not come second to it, or else what was the point of the years of lessons preparing her for that very thing?

The king already thought of his heir as a disappointment, and she didn't want to make that any worse.

She didn't really have a way to make it *better* beyond suffering through training sessions in the courtyard having the sword handed back every few minutes by an irritated Matthew. It was easiest to pour over trade records and recent history, taking as detailed notes as she could and going back over them to consider what she would do in such a situation - or by talking to Ezekiel whenever he wasn't working as a guard, getting his thoughts on the world from the perspective of someone from outside of Dunatel.

So that's what she did, spending painful mornings in the courtyard with Matthew and sore afternoons in lessons or in the library with Jasper, or walking outside with him and Ezekiel when the soldier was either off duty or going on a training run, where he'd stop and do push-ups or run through drills after every lap of the castle wall.

It was a late afternoon, really closer to sunset than anything else, when she found Jasper in his spot by the usual window, but on the desk across from him where she usually sat was a neat pile of manuscripts and a pair of scrolls.

"What's this?" Nadia asked, sitting with a frown to look

down at them.

"Those are the records of people like you," he said simply, not looking up from the pages he was reading through. "Those scrolls are written by me, all stories that used to be word of mouth. The rest is a compilation of pages I was able to pull from census records regarding a change of names, but since the census has only been around for a decade or so it's not as extensive as it could be."

"O-oh." Nadia had almost forgotten he offered to do that, and she blinked down at them in surprise.

"I kept any personal details out of the stories," Jasper said then, lifting his head. "Since you know, some of their methods appear to be *controversial*."

Magic. Nadia glanced up, finding the library was mostly empty, save for a monk near the back wall and a pair of apprentices transcribing in another corner. She nodded anyway, picking up one of the pages to read over name corrections curiously.

"I'll keep them with my personal things anyway," she promised softly. "Th-thank you for this."

"You're welcome."

"I didn't know anyone else felt this way," Nadia admitted. "Until you mentioned all of this." Was she really not... bizarre? It seemed too good to be true when he first said it, and now he'd brought her *proof*. Of course he had. This was Jasper.

"With the number of people that exist just within Cidon, let alone all of Ardenia and the lands around us, it's not very likely to be the only person to feel some way," Jasper said matter of factly. "Obviously it *can* happen, and obviously there's so many other factors to put into that, but... but you're not the only one."

There was some kind of comfort in how he said it like any other one of his facts, something that had always been true but Nadia just hadn't known it. She'd need to thank the stars next time she was in the temple to pray because even if they'd put her in a place where she felt miserable, they'd also put Jasper right beside her.

"What would I do without you, Jasper?"

"You'd know fewer things, but I don't know how different your overall life would be." Jasper shrugged. "Have you thought any more about what you're going to do?"

"Do?" Nadia almost laughed, sitting back with a sigh. "Nothing, probably. I... I don't even know what I'd do or how to go about that. Maybe once I read through these, but even then..."

"Whatever you want to do, I'll try to help you." Jasper folded his hands on the table, though one finger still tapped on the surface. "I'm sure we could figure something out."

"You could, if I actually knew what I wanted." Nadia agreed. It seemed like a problem with no real solution, and maybe focusing on it would just make everything more difficult. She was supposed to be focusing on just about *anything* but that. She was supposed to be focusing on becoming a good ruler.

Jasper had put in the effort to collect these for her, though, so Nadia pulled open a scroll and read through the story, the description of a young person wanting to be seen differently, and the ways they'd found to make it happen.

A seamstress who didn't mind adjusting clothes for body types, for people who just wanted to try something different. An herbalist or the owner of an apothecary that, somehow, had a salve that could slowly start to change how the world saw you. Dozens of thinly veiled descriptions of illegal magic, hidden in medicine or cosmetics, with all the names and locations tactfully left out or clearly changed by Jasper's transcription, and Nadia couldn't help but feel curious.

Magic had been outlawed since King Arthur took the throne generations ago. The reasoning was danger, unpredictability, and the inherent evil that those who used magic invited into their hearts. She'd never even *seen* magic before, so Nadia wasn't sure what to think of that, but the descriptions *here* only mentioned helpfulness and utility.

"These are all just stories you've heard from people?" She asked curiously, glancing up at Jasper as he pored over his own reading. He looked up with a frown and nodded.

"My sister hears more, she works in the textile shop and is better with people than I am," he explained. "But she likes to tell me about all the ma- all the gossip when I visit, whenever she tells me about this kind of thing I remember it because it's very interesting, and those are the details I've remembered."

He had an excellent memory, so Nadia figured if the gossip his sister heard was accurate so were the things written here. She hadn't realized how interested he was in magic, but it was starting to seem that Nadia hadn't realized a few things about Jasper until recently. She needed to work more on what Ezekiel had suggested to her - on 'looking outside' herself.

"What do you think of it?" Jasper asked. "Of the stories, of the... the methods?"

"I think I wish magic wasn't illegal." Nadia chuckled, shaking her head. "I don't know, I suppose there's reason enough to be wary of it. But anything can be dangerous if used wrong, right? Like a sword or even a rock or a plate, *if* you throw it at someone or stab someone it's dangerous."

"But left alone, it's just there." Jasper nodded thoughtfully.

"I see."

"What do you think?" Nadia knew Jasper had studied everything about the world he could, so she could only imagine magic was included in that if he was truly this curious about it. "Do you think these stories are true, there's still casters out there?"

"I don't know," he glanced around again at the near-empty library and lowered his voice to a whisper even she could barely hear. "We probably shouldn't talk about *that* here, even if you are the heir. I... I'm not protected like you."

"Oh, yeah." That was easy to forget, spending so much time in her own head, Nadia was forgetting that other people thought differently - including her own father, who had a penchant for violence to solve any problems. It wasn't even suspicion, *everyone* knew that a magic user would be executed upon discovery.

"We can talk later, I'll go up to your chambers after dinner." Jasper offered quietly.

"Alright," that might be for the best, even though nobody but her personal maids were really supposed to go into her rooms. Nobody paid that much attention to Jasper, so he would be alright. "I'll see you then."

* * *

"If you were able to find a way," Jasper stood by her window, arms folded with his fingers tapping their usual rhythm. "Would you want to actually change?"

"I..." and that was the problem, wasn't it, because the answer to that was yes in every scenario. She couldn't start thinking that way, or it would just hurt more because she *couldn't*. "Of course I would."

"So why-" Jasper seemed frustrated, as he usually did when he didn't quite understand something. "You're literally the *heir to the throne*, Nadia. If anyone could convince the king to make a change, make something legal again, or even give just you a pass on it, it's you. Why don't you explain to him, get permission to go off and find one of these casters?"

"So you think they're real?" Nadia asked, and Jasper nodded.

"I'm positive. Making something illegal doesn't make that thing stop existing, even if it's really rare these days." He cleared his throat. "When the old King Arthur banned magic, a *lot* of the casters were executed for it. And since then, not very many have shown up. None, in official records, but... in less official, there's whispers." He gestured to the scrolls on the bookshelf. "Whispers of people who use it to *help*. To help people like you *and* other simpler day-to-day needs. To heal, or provide food or shelter, or make crops grow... it's *useful*. If you could just-"

"Once I'm king, I could change the laws," Nadia said. "But asking my father to do it is..." crazy, impossible, a good way to get herself punished or even *hurt*. She shook her head, head full of all the ways she'd already failed as an heir. "King Richard is not someone who takes advice. Especially not from me."

"He's your *father*," Jasper protested. "You're the *heir*. Have you even tried?" He didn't understand, it was almost impossible for him to understand. Jasper's interactions with the king were only ever professional, and brief. He had no idea the way King Richard felt about Nadia.

"Not this specifically," Nadia shrugged. The only thing she'd done right, in her father's eyes, was being born as a boy. What would he even say if she brought this up to him? "I can- I can always try, I *guess*, if it was more important. But it's just what I want, it's not better for the kingdom for me to feel like myself."

"I don't think that's true." Jasper turned to face her, then gestured toward one wall, where a mirror she hated sat. "Look, Nadia, look at yourself. If you can't even be the *person* you want to be, how can you be the *ruler* you want to be?"

"That's not the same thing."

Nadia turned anyway, taking in the reflection of who the whole world thought she was, Prince Lewis, a shut-in and a disappointment but the heir just the same.

"I've been taught my entire life about being a ruler, being a king," Nadia said to the reflection of herself, and the reflection of Jasper standing behind her, and she pulled up her sleeve to expose the heir's tattoo that sat there, and he frowned. "That's what I need to be focusing on, at least right now."

"I don't want your name in history books to be the *wrong one*."

It was almost unlike him, to be focusing so much on a detail of someone else's life. They were *friends*, and Nadia appreciated it even if there wasn't much either of them could do. If it was the records of history he was concerned about, that made sense knowing his search for accuracy.

"It won't be. You- *you* can take the records, we can change it when it's a better time, I... I can't tell the king about this, Jasper." She didn't want to have to explain it, she really didn't. Surely Jasper could just accept that this had to be a secret. He hated secrets, and she knew that, but...

"Okay, okay! So don't. If you don't want to, I can't make you. But there's still magic out there that can help you if you go to find it." Jasper said unexpectedly.

"What, run away?" Nadia turned around incredulously, but

Jasper looked completely serious. Of course he did. Jasper didn't generally say things he didn't mean to say. "What's gotten into you, Jasper? Why do you care so much?"

"I-" Jasper sighed, rubbing his eyes. "I just... I want you to be happy, Nadia, you're my best friend. I want the world to see you how I see you, and I want them all to know who you are. If you stay as Prince Lewis to the world, that will never happen."

"It could, I can... I can be a good person, a good ruler, I can change the world as Prince Lewis." She had no other choice. Born into this station, Nadia would either change the world in a good way or a bad way, and she wanted it to be good.

"But every time someone calls you that, I see you get *upset*," Jasper said. "I'm not... not good with feelings, Nadia, but I know you. And it hurts you, and..."

"I appreciate your concern," Nadia took a deep breath. "But right now, I just- I need to focus on what's important."

"*You're* important." Jasper closed his eyes, taking a step back. "I- I don't want to argue with you, I'm... I just don't like seeing you upset."

"And I don't like *being* upset," Nadia admitted. "But right now, at least, this is all we can do."

"Will you at least think about options?" Jasper asked softly. "Will you at least think that maybe you could be *yourself*, and be happy? Please?"

"I-" This was Jasper. He was just asking her to think about something, he wasn't even really trying to get her to do anything. It was *Jasper*. Acting... different, in a way she didn't usually see him, but it was still *Jasper*. "I'll think about it."

"Good." Jasper straightened his posture and stepped back further toward the door. "I should- it's late, I should be leaving,

I'm not technically supposed to come in here. Goodnight, Nadia."

Well, that was bizarre. What had gotten into him today?

"Goodnight." She turned to watch him go, a satchel of books at his side and hands fidgeting with the shoulder strap to it, and then a moment later she was alone again.

Alone in a room for someone she wasn't, with a mirror that reflected a stranger back, and some sick feeling on her skin telling her everything was just *wrong*. It made her feel nauseous to even look at herself, but that had always been the case.

Stars above, why did Jasper have to care so much? This would all be easier if she'd never told him, if she'd just dealt with it herself and was able to stop thinking about it. As wonderful as it felt for him to use *her* name, as wonderful as it felt to be seen as *herself* by even one person, Nadia had no idea what to do now that she wished the whole world knew.

He was right about that, as he was with just about everything. Having her reign in history books as 'King Lewis' would hurt for her entire life, and quite possibly keep her spirit restless and ghostly when she died. What was she supposed to do?

It just about sounded like she had three options, and all of them sounded like hell on earth if she really thought about it.

One choice would be to continue on as she was, keeping this all to herself and becoming exactly what everyone expected, a king. Maybe then, later, she could think about this again… but only the stars knew when that would be. *Was it sacrilege, maybe, to hate the body the stars had given her?*

Another would be to try to ask her father, the current king, to allow her to go off and find a caster to help her change - or even, really, just tell him and change what she could on her own.

The King already saw Nadia as weak, and she honestly thought that if her mother had any other children before her death they would be chosen as the heir rather than Nadia despite her being the firstborn. So who knows what he would even say to this, what he would do, or what might happen then.

Then the third option, Jasper had suggested she just go off and find a caster herself, abandon the castle and her lessons and preparations and everything she'd ever really known.

That sounded terrifying, and again there was the worry of what King Richard's response would be. Part of her thought he wouldn't even notice, but if he was truly planning a marriage treaty then he might be paying more attention to her than usual even if it was just a subconscious thing.

Oh, she just wanted to fall asleep and stop having to think about this for a few hours, it's not like a decision was going to be made tonight anyway. It had been far too long of a day, the sun was already far gone and even resting on the windowsill to look at the stars didn't cheer her up the way they usually did.

Nadia drew the curtains, avoided looking in the mirror, and only kept one lamp lit to take her hair down and change into something more comfortable for sleeping.

Tomorrow would be better, or it would be the same, but she couldn't imagine tomorrow being any *worse*.

6

The Truth

"So what do you do all day anyway, Prince, up in that castle of yours?"

It was another afternoon when Jasper had taken time off from scholar work and invited her to walk with him and Ezekiel around the walls and gardens of the castle. Nadia had been enjoying it, for the most part, it was always interesting to hear what Ezekiel had to say even if he was usually talking to Jasper, and she was just listening because there wasn't much else to do.

"It's not all that fun," she said now, to his question. "A lot of- of research, some training, for the most part. And studying with Jasper in the library."

"Well, I knew that part." Ezekiel grinned. "Jasper mentions it enough, I'd be crazy to forget."

"I don't mention it all that often," Jasper protested. "I talk about a *lot* of things, why shouldn't our heir be one of them? You're also an artist, Lewis, you're really good!"

"Wh- I wouldn't say that," Nadia winced, but Ezekiel only seemed more curious. "Well you know, some people say that-

that drawing or practicing calligraphy helps with- with your swordsmanship. It hasn't helped *me* much, but I still enjoy it."

"What do you draw?" Ezekiel asked, pausing to drop to the ground and do push-ups.

"People, mostly. Scholars in the library, or- or servants and stuff. Anyone I see, I suppose. I just enjoy it."

"An Artist King, then," Ezekiel jumped up from his push-ups, and Nadia blinked in surprise. "Not much like King Richard, are you?"

Well- that was *rude*.

"What do you and other soldiers do all day?" Nadia returned the question instead of indulging his insult. "I can only imagine your life is different than mine is."

"Well, there's always training to be done." Ezekiel picked up a stone to toss between his hands. "But that only takes up a few hours a day, to keep us ready for the springtime. Depending on your skill set and your assignment, there are differences. Some are employed as city or castle guards when we're at home, that's actually what I did for a few years before I enlisted to fight in Rasnia."

"I see." *How long ago had he left his family and come out here, then? He couldn't be much older than Nadia and Jasper were.*

"I've recently been spending time in the barracks with our wounded men, helping where I can, but winter always gets a bit dull, doesn't it? There's just less to do except wait for spring to come, no matter what your profession is."

"My parents have great business in the winter, actually," Jasper piped up. "New clothes help against the cold, and theirs are some of the best."

"Okay, well, that's an exception." Ezekiel laughed. *"Most*

professions slow down, I wasn't being completely literal." At that, Jasper simply looked betrayed.

"*Why?*"

"I was close enough! You all knew what I meant, didn't you?"

"No, because you made a general statement when you knew it wasn't true for everything," Jasper said stubbornly - probably just to make a point, as Nadia knew he could read between the lines if he really wanted to. "How would we know what you meant if you didn't say it? Honestly, you're *just* as bad as Lewis is."

"I still don't remember when scholars gained the station to use royalty's first names," Ezekiel said - it was a comment he made almost every time Jasper used her birth name. "Just because you think you're smarter than everyone else doesn't mean you're above respect, Jasper."

"I said you could call me whatever you want, too," Nadia reminded him, pushing down the nausea brought out by her real name. "That's not Jasper's fault."

"Yeah, that's not my fault! And I don't think I'm smarter than *everyone* else, just... most other people."

Oh, well, *that* might not be true at all, but Nadia kept it to herself while Ezekiel sputtered disagreements. If anyone in the world should think highly of himself, it would be Jasper.

"Did you really mean that?" Ezekiel turned to Nadia, having exhausted his attempts at getting Jasper to admit he was a bit full of himself. "That I could call you by just your name?"

"Of course," Nadia shrugged. "Why would I say something if I didn't mean it?"

"Oh, not this *again.*"

"Yeah, and *you* say things you don't mean all the time, Lewis," Jasper added. "I see right through you, nice try."

"I feel like you could see right through anyone if you tried," Ezekiel remarked. "Even if you pretend not to. You're very observant, J, *and* really smart."

"What? I don't *pretend* anything! Being observant doesn't mean I understand what people are thinking," Jasper said defensively. "But with Nadia, I know because we're best friends."

"Who's Nadia?"

Damnit. Jasper had almost slipped up a few times in front of other people over the past week or so, but he'd always caught himself before he really said anything obvious. It had been too good to last for so long, and she should have known that. She was never lucky for very long.

"Did I say *Nadia*? I-I don't think I did," Jasper stammered, shaking his head. "No, um... I definitely said... something else."

"Oh yeah? What did you say then?" Ezekiel pressed, and Nadia couldn't help but wince sympathetically at Jasper's panicked, fidgeting hands. Oh, she hadn't wanted to put him in any situations like this... she never should have told him the truth, no matter how nice it had been.

"I said- I said somebody," Jasper attempted, somehow pronouncing the word 'somebody' wrong enough that it almost sounded like it could have been confused. Nadia might have laughed at his attempts if this didn't put them both in such a precarious situation.

"You're a terrible liar, J, you know that right?" Ezekiel had stopped in his tracks, a deep frown taking over his face as he turned to her. "How about we do that honesty thing again, Prince? Be blunt - do *you* know who he's talking about?"

She could either lie, which would only delay the inevitable

and possibly hurt whatever the relationship between Jasper and Ezekiel was - or she could just be honest and hope that Jasper could convince him to keep it quiet. From what she'd seen so far, Jasper was very good at convincing Ezekiel of things.

She could still be vague, though.

"Yes, I do know." Nadia sighed, while Jasper sent her an apologetic look from behind Ezekiel's shoulder. "Not someone you should worry about, Ezekiel, I think he likes you more."

"That- okay, that's not..." *he* was flustered now, and it was almost entertaining as he backtracked. "I'm just confused, Jasper, you've never mentioned someone named Nadia before. Who is she?"

"That- well, it's a long story and it's complicated and I'm- I.." Jasper grimaced. "I've been asked not to talk about it..."

"It's alright," Nadia said, humming for a moment while she looked over Ezekiel's face. She'd enjoyed their interactions so far, and he seemed to be a good person *and* Jasper seemed to trust him. "Do you really want to know, Ezekiel?"

"That's *why* I was asking."

Nadia hummed thoughtfully, taking a careful look at their surroundings. Nobody else was around, they were halfway around the back of the castle wall and even the guards on top of it couldn't hear their voices from that high.

"Nadia is the name I'd rather have, it's just *me*." She admitted. "Jasper is only keeping that from you because I asked him, there's no reason to trust him any less."

"What?"

"You asked me to be honest." Nadia shrugged. There was something exhilarating about being able to tell people this- even if it had only been Jasper so far, it had been such a *relief* to say it even if it was terrifying. Hopefully, she could get Ezekiel to understand the same way Jasper had.

"But- okay, but what does that *mean*? 'Nadia' is hardly a- oh, wait a minute..." So he wasn't an idiot, Nadia had already figured that if he was close with Jasper.

"I didn't mean to," Jasper said quietly once again, and Nadia just shook her head.

"I'm the one who told you, I know you're not very good at keeping information to yourself." It was too late now anyway, she only hoped that Ezekiel would be understanding.

"I-I could be! I'd try, for you..."

"So you- hold on," Ezekiel protested, holding up his hands. "You're one of those- those people who want to be *different*. Right?"

"Seems that way," Nadia sighed. "Not too different, but... yes."

"Why? You- you're royalty, you get basically anything you want already. There- there's nothing better for you as a woman than you'd get as a man, if anything I can only see life being harder for you. So why are- I don't get it."

"Have you never felt like you just aren't quite the person you're supposed to be?" That sounded dumb. *Oh, no*, she was messing this up. What if Ezekiel didn't agree to keep it quiet? "I can't really tell you why, I can only tell you that I'd feel better as a princess than a prince, but..." another glance around, and they were still alone. "But you're right, it would complicate my life quite a bit. That's why nobody knows but Jasper, and now you."

He was a loyal soldier- surely she could convince him to keep this to himself. If anything else, she could order him to even if that might make him dislike her even more than he already did.

"Please don't tell anyone, Ez, I promised..." Jasper wrung his hands together as he spoke. "It- it's not so big a deal, anyway, it's her own life."

"I... of course, I wouldn't tell a soul." Ezekiel took a slow breath, and it was interesting to watch someone think when they didn't do it quite as quickly as Jasper did.

She could all but see his mind working while he squinted at her... but he *was* saying he would keep her secret. *Thank the stars.*

"You're the heir to the throne, I'm loyal to you, and- and there would be no reason for me to tell anyone about this anyway. *And-* and even if you weren't the heir, Jasper cares about you so I'd keep any secret you ask of me. But I-I don't really *understand.*"

"I don't really know how to explain it." Nadia laughed weakly. "So that's perfectly fine, I appreciate your discretion."

"Is this why you stay inside all day, then? It's because you don't want to be seen- seen as you are now?" Ezekiel asked curiously.

"Not really, at least not completely," Nadia said as they started on their walk once again. "I just never really thought to try and leave, not for years. When I was young it was seen as unsafe, so I wasn't allowed. Now that I'm an adult I never really thought to change that."

"Some people think you're ill, or a bit mad," Ezekiel said. "But you seem *healthy* to me, that's one reason I was curious. If you died we'd have no heir and be in a bad spot, so it made sense if that *was* the reason..."

"I'm not sick, and I'm not mad," Nadia laughed now, surprised to hear such a thing. Did people really think that? He'd mentioned rumors before, but she hadn't realized *that's* what he meant. "I'm just a creature of habit, probably too much. That's Jasper's fault, he's a bad influence on me."

"Hey, no I'm not! Having habits is a good thing." Jasper protested. "It keeps your life organized."

"I was joking," Nadia reassured him, though it only earned her a dramatic frown.

"Jokes are supposed to be funny, you can't just lie and call it a joke, I've told you that a hundred times."

"It's funny *because* it's a lie," Ezekiel explained, though Nadia knew from experience it would change nothing. He probably did too, if the fond look on his face said anything. "Because I know you're not a bad influence on anyone."

"But that's not *funny*." Jasper sighed, committed to being stubborn. "You two are so hard to understand, I don't get it."

"Ah, but you like us anyway." Nadia grinned, and he rolled his eyes with a huff.

"Yeah, I guess I do."

* * *

Long days were turning to longer nights, where no matter how much she wanted to, Nadia just couldn't seem to fall asleep. There was too much to think about, too much to consider, and too much of that strange *wrong* sensation in her chest and under her skin.

Two people knew now, and while she hadn't known Ezekiel for very long his reaction was almost surprising. He didn't understand all that much, from what he'd said, why she would want to be something different unless there was some kind of *advantage*. He'd still agreed to keep it quiet, and he'd even

THE TRUTH

tentatively used the name 'Nadia' for her even though she could tell he didn't like being so informal.

That was fair. Formality was important to most nobles and royals she'd met, but it *was* different for people close to them and Jasper was as close as it got in Nadia's case. So it only made sense that Ezekiel could be given a similar privilege, due to that connection. At least, it made sense to her. Maybe she really was mad, and the rumors were true, and she just hadn't realized it yet. That might explain why some things felt like they were impossible, even when other people acted like they weren't.

Jasper had asked her why she didn't at least try talking to her father, to the king, about what was going on. He didn't know the king's temperament very well, but *maybe* he had a point.

If two people in the world didn't hate her for this, perhaps a third would be just as understanding. Was that a risk she could even take? Who knows what King Richard would do or say if he found it unacceptable?

Was the risk of him disapproving stronger than the *relief* she'd feel if he let her find some way to act on this? Even if he was like Ezekiel, and didn't understand, maybe he *would* still let her do this. Just because she was a disappointment to him didn't mean he'd hate her so outright, surely...

Too restless to sleep, Nadia pulled herself up to pace around the room, turning the possibilities around in her head in some attempt to either wear herself out or make a decision on it.

What would she even do, if he gave the pardon to let her find some caster and actually change? Sure, she might not need magic if she could just change wardrobe which would honestly be incredible in its own right - but truly *changing* in some ways was something she'd only thought of in actual dreams, never in reality. Never until Jasper had brought magic into the equation with his stories and understanding.

Thinking of good possibilities rested on the very strong *if* of whether or not the king would react well or react terribly, and thinking about them too much might just make it hurt worse if they never happened at all.

Oh, why was she torturing herself by thinking about this *all the time*? Why couldn't she just exist normally, either born how she felt or feeling the way she was born? It would certainly be easier if the universe had just gone along with how her heart was beating.

A few weeks ago, telling anyone about this at all seemed like the craziest thing she could do. Now, two people knew and had either accepted her outright or at least agreed it was her own life to live. That would be a cruel joke of the stars to play on her - if they were the odd ones out.

The room she was pacing in, although spacious, suddenly felt far too small for the complicated fear coursing through her. She certainly wasn't getting to sleep anytime soon, so Nadia relented and pulled on a spare pair of shoes before slipping out into the dark corridors of the castle to wander instead.

It wouldn't be the first time, but it had been a few years since she gave into the childish urge to ramble through the castle in the dead of night. The small number of staff that worked into the evenings and nights wouldn't be bothered or surprised, and maybe one of the maids would give her some kind of menial task to do to keep her busy until she got tired enough to rest. They'd done it before, and as repetitive as some chores could be, anything might be better than letting herself get lost in the possibilities of the future.

Alas, the corridors were all but deserted and she only found herself thinking about more and more possibilities as the minutes dragged by, so much that she'd exhausted the center tower and wandered into less-used hallways and rooms that were only used to entertain guests or hold meetings, none of which were happening any time soon.

She must have been pacing for over an hour, well past midnight, by the time a light flickered at the end of a corridor, coming from under the door to an office that, as far as she knew, hadn't been used in years if not decades. Curious, and desperate for anything to focus on other than herself, Nadia walked down along one wall, letting her elbow rub against the bricks just to feel the skin tug and rub uncomfortably.

Low voices came from within, one she knew was her fathers and the other two were a general and the swordmaster Matthew. That was... odd. Why would they be talking here, in some random small clerk's office in the emptiest hallways? Why would they be talking at the latest hours of the night, as well?

"Are you sure about this course of action, my liege?" The first asked, and Nadia paused outside the door, leaning on the wall with one shoulder as she listened. Why were they here in some random office, why so late? What was going- "He's the *heir*."

Oh, were they talking about her? Nadia frowned, bringing a hand up over her mouth to stay quiet. She'd been trying so hard not to mess up recently, and she thought she'd been doing a good job - so why on earth would they be talking about her?

"Once he's married, we'll have more options that way," Richard said dismissively. "Whether they have a child quickly or not, *their* family is much larger than ours."

"More than half the citizens already gossip that he's as sickly as his mother," Matthew added eagerly. "So him falling ill and dying soon after marriage will simply be a tragedy, but not any kind of surprise. All the path has been laid for us, *this is the right time,* my King."

What?

"I still don't see why killing him-" the general was cut off.

"If that boy ever tries to rule this kingdom, Cidon would crumble to dust." The king snapped.

He sounded irritated, in a tone Nadia knew all too well. As if he was tired of explaining the same thing over and over again. *How often had he talked about this?*

"He takes too much after his mother, he's too soft. I'd rather adopt the Oceans into our royal family than leave it to him. And don't forget, advancing on Rasnia from the south and the ocean will make it easier to finish this war for the both of us if we're truly united."

None of this made any *sense*. Nadia blinked harshly, as if that would get her brain to start working properly, but all it did was make her father's casual, evil words drill into her head even further.

What had been those thoughts not hours ago, that perhaps she'd underestimated the care the king held for his only child? What had been that idea that maybe he would let her exist freely as she wished, if she told him how she felt?

What had been that idea Jasper proposed, of *running* and not telling anyone where she'd gone or why she'd left?

7

Trust

Even on the best days, Nadia sat numbly, disconnected from the world around her. It was easier when she was with Jasper, and Ezekiel now to some extent - and it was easier when she could read or draw and listen to Jasper talk about his research and studies.

Now, waking up groggy after her discovery the night before, the usual cloud that sat in Nadia's mind overwhelmed her completely. Part of her desperately wanted to believe it had all been a dream, but the things she'd heard were undeniable, and even after sleeping it was impossible to tell herself it hadn't been real.

Her father wanted her *dead*. In some ways, she'd already believed that - he said before that any other heir would have been better, so she could fill in the dots. But...

Last night he'd *said* it. Last night she'd heard him *planning* it. He wanted her dead so badly he was actually going to kill her, and he was going to use it to unravel a centuries-old alliance between the three kingdoms.

No amount of reading could push that out of her head, no

matter which old childhood storybook she dug out of her trunks and shelves to try and lose herself in. No detailed drawing was enough for her to get lost in the lines and shadows of a face or figure, all of it just made her think of darkness and secrets and death.

Anything she could think of, to get her father's words out of her head, Nadia tried. It didn't work.

They repeated back and forth in her mind, and no matter what she did or told herself it didn't feel like anything other than reality.

Some of what he'd said, in the safety of darkness and closed doors and rooms that were never used or even regularly cleaned... he'd been safe to speak his mind, and so some of the things Nadia heard could only be *facts*. As much as she wanted to reject them, she'd spent far too much time with scholars like Jasper to be able to do that.

It was simply a fact that her father was only marrying the Oceans into their family so they'd still have an heir when he killed her. To solidify a treaty *not* meant to end the war, but to turn on their allies northward and take *their* kingdom, breaking the alliance of three kingdoms that had existed for hundreds and hundreds of years. To drag on a war even further that had cost hundreds of lives, and would surely cost hundreds more... and she'd always had so many questions about why the war couldn't end, only to be shut out from the meetings.

Of *course* she wasn't allowed in meetings of the war, of *course* he would refuse that even when he constantly complained that she didn't follow in his footsteps. If these were his plans, there was no future where staying here and pretending to be a prince would help her become a great ruler.

If these were his plans, there was no *future* at all.

What on earth was she meant to *do*? She could run, sure, but where? The stories of magic Jasper had told her were only rumors, and Nadia had never traveled on her own and even then, those trips to the coastal cities had been years and years ago when she was only a child. Even if she did run off, find a caster, and ask them to help her, what would she do after that? Could she find a way to stop her father's plot against Rasnia? Not *currently*, not with the way she was so much weaker than he was.

She'd never thought so much about her own death, why would she?

"Jasper," Nadia hadn't even meant to speak, but she was so glad to see Jasper after a day of training with Matthew where she had to pretend she hadn't heard him the night before, and lessons where she fought to keep herself awake while they went over politics and diplomacy and economics that she'd need if she ever got to rule this kingdom.

What a terrible thought, she might never have to use those skills at all.

"Good afternoon," Jasper took her arrival as a cue to break from his writings, quill settled onto the desk as he stretched. The library was almost empty, but he was here - as he was almost always when he wasn't off with Ezekiel. "I've been wondering when you'd get here, I found something *fascinating* about the way people's language and words develop over time. Linguistics has never been my area of study, but I can't say it isn't something worth a lot of time. I might take a few weeks and read more into it if I'm not too busy."

"That's wonderful," Nadia couldn't help but smile, sinking down into her chair. He always brought more clarity to her world, and today that was one thing Nadia needed more than anything else.

"It really is! Did you know that until a hundred years ago, everyone said 'lights' instead of 'stars' when they were talking about the gods? We had the word stars, and the word lights, and everyone knew it meant stars. But until the past few decades, everyone just called them 'lights' for some reason. I think the change originated when a poem was published and became a nursery rhyme and *it* called them stars, and then it spread- but I'm not completely sure yet."

He was going to talk about this for an hour if she let him, and part of her wanted to. Nadia had actual questions for him today, though, and her chest felt too tight to truly enjoy what he was saying.

"Jasper do- do you remember what you asked me to think about?" She asked when he paused for breath.

"I usually ask you to think about everything, since thinking is far better than not thinking." Jasper nodded. "But I- I know what you're talking about."

"I want to go," Nadia whispered, glancing around them. The room *was* almost empty, though there could be a scholar or two hidden in the shelves in search of whatever their study was. "I-I need you to tell me *where* those stories happened."

"What?" Jasper sat upright, eyes wide. "You want- what, to... to find them?"

How was she supposed to explain that she'd overheard, how there would be no chance in the future to change later if she stayed here? That was too much, it was too complicated, it sounded too impossible.

"I-I want to do what you said," Nadia shrugged weakly. "I want to be me, and I want to be happy."

And she didn't want to *die*.

That was her only plan right now, the rest could come later. Being a queen, saving the soldiers and the treaty and her kingdom- all of that had to come later. Nadia couldn't lead anyone into peace if she was dead.

"Okay," Jasper nodded thoughtfully, reaching up to push his hair away from his eyes. "I.. I do know the area where those stories come from. There's one, *mostly*, but some come from everywhere. But we- we shouldn't talk about it here. Are you alright?"

"Yeah, I just... I've just been thinking a lot," It wasn't an outright lie... she *had* been thinking a lot. It just also wasn't the most important reason. "As long as I can do this, I'll be alright."

"As long as *we* can do this." Jasper corrected her. "I'm not letting you just go on your own, what kind of friend would I be if I just gave you a location and waved you off?"

"You want to come with me?" For some reason, Nadia hadn't even thought of that.

Jasper's entire life was here, he was a royal scholar and if he disappeared that could all very well go away. His family was here - his parents and his sister... not to mention Ezekiel, who Nadia was positive at this point was someone closer to Jasper than just a 'good friend'.

"Of course I do."

* * *

"This is Ardenia."

Jasper unrolled the large scroll across the top of her dresser, which had been cleared of candlesticks and books and other knick knacks Nadia had gathered through her life and left there with nowhere else to put them. They were all now stuffed onto other shelves or into drawers, giving him the space to put the map.

"This bit here is Cidon," he continued, pointing to the center of Ardenia. "Cidon was the first to ban magic, but Rasnia was soon to follow. Ashan is a bit different, they don't have it *banned* but it is pretty taboo anyway, and since then the number of casters has gone down significantly in records as far as I know."

"Okay,"

"That could be just because legends of magic have stopped being spread, so it sounds less common. Casters could just be extremely uncommon." Jasper shrugged. "But what matters to us, for this, is where the current stories of magic in *Cidon* come from."

"You said you *knew*."

"I do," Jasper huffed. "Just listen, I'm getting there."

"Alright, alright," Nadia rolled her eyes and leaned over the map herself, frowning down at the dotted lines of their territories. She knew it almost as well as Jasper did, but hearing him explain things was so *grounding* - and he knew more about magic than she did, apparently. "Go on then."

"Now, the three western territories are all either full of towns or farming, with less farming in the north due to logging operations and the dangers of the forest," Jasper explained. "But the Eastern Mountains have hardly been settled at all - there's only one real town in the mountains these days. *That's* where stories of magic come from."

"All the way there, on the other side of the lake?" Nadia frowned. "How far is that?"

"At least a few weeks' journey, especially since we'd need to go around the water instead of in a straight line. But every story, at least anything with details or credibility, says there are casters in the mountains." Jasper said. "What do you know of politics in Ridgeport?"

"Weak, or nonexistent." Nadia folded her arms as she thought back. "Fewer people to represent, so as far as I recall there's only one noble family there at all and I've never even met them, they never attended councils or balls before the war, and since it started... I don't know. Mining in the mountains was far too difficult, and infrastructure almost impossible - there are suitable mines in the southern hills so there's no real *point* in pushing further east."

"Any rebellions against the current royal family that have ever happened, which aren't many, have come from Ridgeport or surrounding settlements." Jasper placed a finger on the small mark drawn onto the map. "But they *usually* keep to themselves, which makes it a perfect place for someone practicing magic to hide."

"So you think that's where we should go?" She'd never been there- and King Richard hardly ever thought of Ridgeport in the first place, so it wasn't likely that anyone would think to look for her there, as long as she could get away from any of her father's men and lose them on the way.

"If you actually want to leave and find magic, that's the best place to go. Unless you want to travel all the way to Ashan, but that's more of a risk. Ashan keeps to themselves more than Cidon and Rasnia do. They haven't *banned* magic, but they also keep their records more secretive so I haven't been able to get access to them here." He seemed so confident about it, and Jasper was usually confident, but with something as obscure as magic...

"You know more about this than I expected." She admitted, stepping back to sigh, and rubbing her eyes. "How long have you been interested in all this stuff?"

"Magic is illegal, Nadia. Most records of it have been destroyed or turned into nothing but fairy tales, and even those ones are rare." Jasper said grimly, and it wasn't even a real answer was it? "Researching it is difficult and dangerous, but I have to- I *want* to know *everything*. I probably know more than most people- just... just because I've been able to get my hands on certain records that aren't technically supposed to exist."

"Oh." Nadia tilted her head, surprised to hear that he'd put real effort into studying something without rambling about it to her. He was pretty bad at keeping secrets, but he'd somehow avoided ever mentioning this?

"Nadia, I- I could be killed for learning what I've learned," Jasper said in response to her curious look. "You know that, right?"

"*Oh.*" Of course she knew that the penalty for *using* magic was death, but just learning about it? Was the King really so brutal?

Ah, well... Why was she having to flee in the first place? Maybe the reason Jasper was so bad at secrets was because he put all his effort into this one, to avoid the same fate Nadia was fleeing now.

"You won't be killed." Nadia took a deep breath. "This information is as safe with me as it could be with anyone, I trust you."

"Stories, even spoken as fiction, often contain truths." Jasper continued. "And being here in the castle all the time you wouldn't know of all the tales there are about the mountains.

Dragons, beasts, evil casters, and denouncers of gods... not all of them are good stories. The ones I gave you relate to what you're going through, but there's so much *more* than that."

"Well, if the trip takes a few weeks you'll have time to tell me in a place where it's at least a bit safer to." Nadia reasoned. "When's the soonest you think we can leave?"

"I-I mean, if you want to do it really soon I'm not sure," Jasper tapped his fingers lightly onto the map. "We'd need to make sure we have supplies of some kind, warm clothes and shoes, and some food for a trip to the next town over."

"Oh, right." Nadia hadn't thought much of this through, had she, except for the fact that she needed to leave the castle as soon as possible. "I-I'm not sure what all we'd need."

"I can put a list together, I've never traveled much but it can't be all *that* complicated." Jasper shrugged. "We'd just need to be sure to pack well, and then pick a time and method of leaving."

"Right, right," oh, Nadia wasn't thinking well at all today, she was too tired and frazzled from this. "Um..."

"Are you *alright*? You're not acting like yourself."

"I'm fine, I just- I just need to get out of here, I need to find these people who can help me and..." Oh, she wasn't making any sense. "Sorry, I guess I- I haven't slept well."

"How about this," Jasper picked up the map, rolling it back into the scroll he'd carried it here as. "We sleep now, it's late. We need to think this through, Nadia, if we want to be able to find them."

"I know." He was right, as usual.

"I'll do some research tomorrow while you're training and in your lessons, and tomorrow night we can ask Ezekiel for advice."

"Wh- wait, hold on, nobody can *know* where we're going."

Nadia protested. "They'd send someone after us, I'm not supposed to leave the *castle*, let alone the town."

"I can't just leave and *not* tell Ezekiel where I'm going," Jasper scoffed. "He'd worry, I can't do that. And he knows more about traveling than either of us even if he's only been as far east as Stonewell, he's been closer."

"But-"

"Ezekiel wouldn't tell anyone about this if I asked him to keep it a secret," Jasper said easily. "You can trust him, Nadia. And if not, you *just* said you trust me, so trust me!"

"I do trust you."

"So let me talk to him about this, he'll listen to me and he can at least give us some advice for what this kind of trip will take." Jasper insisted. "He's as loyal as they come to the royal family, he wouldn't do anything against you."

That was the problem, wasn't it? Because King Richard was part of the royal family too, and Nadia didn't know whether or not that loyalty would override his apparent devotion to Jasper. She didn't know him well enough.

"Do *you* trust him?"

"I- I tell him *everything*," Jasper said. "If you really want me to keep this, us leaving, a secret? I'll try. But I'll feel really bad about it. Let me do this for you, let me get his help."

Nadia knew he was bad at keeping secrets from Ezekiel, that much was obvious by the one thing she'd already asked him to keep quiet. The good thing is that Ezekiel hadn't told anyone else, and Jasper trusted him.

This was Jasper.

Jasper.

This was her best friend, and if *he* trusted Ezekiel, then Nadia had to trust him on that or she'd get absolutely nowhere.

"Alright." She rubbed her eyes again, and Jasper nodded decisively. "But nobody else, Jasper, *please*."

"I swear it," Jasper said. "Just him, and just enough for him to give us advice on it."

"We'll talk more tomorrow, then," though Nadia wasn't sure how much sleep she'd get tonight either, even with how tired she felt. If she was an insomniac before all this, she had no idea how she would be able to get herself to relax now.

She could at least try, and she could hope that Jasper's plan worked out. Other than that, Nadia wasn't sure what she could even do aside from walking out of the castle and just hoping she wouldn't die from the cold or wild animals.

Leaving only to die on the journey would defeat the entire point of leaving to escape being killed by her father. So if she did this, if they really did leave, Nadia needed to actually *make it* to the mountains, make it to a caster, and get their help, and then… Well, then she could figure out what to do next.

She just had to make it that far.

8

Escape

"Good news!" Jasper announced when she found him in the library, which was nearly deserted at noon since most scholars and scribes would be down in the kitchen eating. "Ez wants to come with us and help!"

"What?" It took a moment for Nadia to even put the words together, with the way her exhausted mind was struggling today. She *had* gotten a few hours of sleep, but not nearly enough, and none that weren't disturbed by vague dreams and waking up out of fear

"Ezekiel wants to come with us so we don't 'die in a ditch somewhere,'" Jasper elaborated, using his fingers to put quotes around the statement. "I told him we just needed advice, but he seemed pretty set on it. And he's right, you know, we don't want to die."

"What did you tell him?" Nadia asked skeptically, already overwhelmed at the idea that three entire people knew what she was planning to do.

"Just what we talked about last night," Jasper shrugged. "He said he wants to ask you about it, too, so you can talk to him about it sometime tonight if you want to. But I think this is great! He's actually traveled and everything before, you know?"

"I suppose..." Nadia wasn't sure. On one hand, she didn't know Ezekiel very well. On the other hand, if he left with them there was far less of a chance he could tell anyone where they'd gone or why. That, and he actually had experience traveling through the forests. It actually might be the best-case scenario, at least in this situation. "Is he *sure*?"

"Well I mean, he might try to talk us out of it." Jasper frowned thoughtfully. "But yeah, he seemed pretty set."

Sure enough, that evening when Jasper arrived at her door there was a now familiar soldier a few steps behind him, brow furrowed and arms crossed.

"What on earth are the two of you thinking?" He demanded as soon as the door was shut behind them. "Prince- Nadia, I mean, what do you think the mountains have in store for you *other* than a dangerous journey and death?"

"Magic, hopefully." Not to mention distance between herself and the men who plotted to kill her, but she didn't want to explain any of that when she was still within the walls of the castle. It was dangerous enough planning things here where they might be overheard. Oh, she couldn't breathe, what if someone had already caught on that she knew? *She had to get out of here.*

"Okay, sure," Ezekiel seemed exasperated already, and Jasper rolled out the map once again on top of Nadia's dresser. "Let me rephrase this, Nadia. You're the heir to the throne, and we all already know that the king prefers to keep you in the castle for whatever reason."

"Yes." To keep her isolated, and give fuel to the rumors that she was sickly so when she died, nobody was surprised.

"What would it look like if you just... disappeared? If a scholar from the royal school took you off and disappeared into the mountains with you? Do you have any idea what the punishment for kidnapping or even assisting in a runaway would be when you're caught?"

"I-" she hadn't really thought that, but she hadn't asked Jasper to come along. He'd wanted to, and she wasn't about to say no to his help or company. Maybe she should. Maybe she should leave without him, and just...

"They might accuse him of being an Ochean spy, or accuse *him* of magic or- or something like that. We're in a war right now and even if we're in a stay of combat you still can't just act like people wouldn't *panic*."

"First of all, Jasper doesn't have to come with me." *She* had to leave, but Ezekiel had a point. This was a terrible idea, she'd probably die either way.... Oh, every choice she had here was dangerous. Nadia didn't know what to *do*. Would she rather die at her father's hand, used as a pawn, or at least *try* to die resisting that?

Would she rather die as Prince Lewis, or as Nadia?

"What? Hold on, I *want* to go." Jasper interrupted. "I'm just as curious about magic as you are about getting their help, Nadia. Do you have any idea how much I-I could learn when we find them? Whatever happens, you'd be able to vouch for me to the court, wouldn't you?"

At this point, Nadia wasn't even sure of that even though she'd told Jasper that very thing only days ago. Days ago, she'd thought that her father cared for her the smallest of smallest amounts. Now, Nadia was almost sure that he didn't.

"Well yeah, but I don't want to- to put you or your job here at risk for this, I-"

"Okay, stop. Both of you, stop." Ezekiel held out his hands between them. "Are you thinking this *through*, Nadia? I may be invested in Jasper's safety, but I'm also loyal to *you* and if you die, the Cidon throne is nothing. There are no other heirs, no family, *are you thinking this through?*"

"I'm not going to die." Of course she wasn't thinking this through. Of course she could die. She probably would, whether she left or not. But Nadia didn't know what other chance at a future she *had*. Everyone in this castle felt like an enemy, aside from him and Jasper... and even Ezekiel felt like an enemy, sometimes.

"If you leave here alone? You very well might. The woods between here and Stonewell alone are dangerous, and the further east you go the less help you'd be able to find." Ezekiel stared into her eyes, and Nadia felt horribly like he could just see into her soul and know *everything* that was going on. "If you'd take my advice on this, I'd say not to leave. But you're going to, no matter what, aren't you?" There was no way he knew the truth, was there? He would say so. *Right?*

"Yeah, I am." Nadia steeled herself. "I have to. I know you don't understand, and I shouldn't ask either of you to risk as much as you would be going with me, but-"

"I... would be breaking the oath I took, to protect the throne and the royal family and the people of Cidon, if I knew you were leaving and I let you go alone," Ezekiel said slowly. "So if you go, I go. And if Jasper goes, I go. Are you *sure* you want to go, J?" Part of Nadia thought that Ezekiel was insisting on coming mostly for Jasper's sake, but including Nadia in his explanation was a kind gesture anyway.

"Positive." Jasper nodded stubbornly.

"So it's all three of us, or I'll find some way to keep you here." he folded his arms again. "I don't think this is a good idea, but if you're set on it, I'm going. And I can tell you're going either way, Prince."

That didn't make sense- why was he agreeing this easily? Why had he accepted it so quickly, after all the good points he made? Nadia stared at him, but Ezekiel had broken eye contact with her and was now looking at Jasper as if this was the most normal thing in the world.

"So that's that, then." Jasper cleared his throat. "I told you she was serious, Ez. We're all going, and you know the most about this kind of thing. What can you tell us about the best way to the mountains?"

Ezekiel sighed and turned to look at the map, and Nadia followed after.

"If you want to keep from being found," Ezekiel said. "Because there *will* be people looking for you, we'd want to keep to smaller roads, and that takes longer. But there's a good enough path between here and Stonewell, I've taken it a few times when I was younger. Once we're there, I know some people who can give us directions into the mountains, to Ridgeport."

"That's where your family lives, right?" Nadia recalled, and the soldier nodded grimly.

"They'll be able to help us, at least a *bit*. I know someone there who excels in subtlety... at least he did, before. But it takes two weeks or so to even *get* to Stonewell, at least on foot. Horseback would be better, but I don't know how we'd sneak out with three entire horses."

"I don't trust horses, anyway," Jasper said. "They always look at me like they *know* something."

"They're just horses, J, we've talked about thi- y'know what, that doesn't matter. We can't get them in the first place, they leave more of a trail and they require more resources, we can go on foot." Ezekiel said thoughtfully. "As far as resources go, the best spot to get more would be six days out in Barcombe, if we wanted to avoid towns and bigger settlements."

"That would probably be best," Nadia admitted. "The less chance of being recognized, the better, I think."

"You won't be easily recognized anyway, aside from people who have been to festivals here in Dunatel," Ezekiel said. "And there *will* be ways to disguise you, especially if Jasper can get commoner's clothes from his sister. *Can* you do that, J?"

"I can try, it shouldn't be too hard. You and she are about the same size, Nadia, so I'm hoping to borrow hers." Jasper shrugged. "Or steal it, she'll be fine. She can just make more."

"Right, right, that sounds... fine," Nadia had forgotten how many of her clothes had some kind of crest or even just nice enough materials that it would make her stick out if she was trying to pass as a commoner.

As skilled as Jasper's family was in making clothes and different textiles, they provided for common folk and lower-class nobles, not royalty. So at a glance, wearing anything they'd made, she wouldn't draw the attention that a prince might.

"Wait, don't- you can't just steal her clothes." Nadia rubbed her eyes, barely processing what Jasper had said. He didn't seem worried, though, and just laughed.

"Sure I can, she has plenty."

"Just-" Ezekiel interrupted, holding up a hand. "Just get some, J, and don't tell us how you did it. Alright?"

"I can go down to visit them anytime." Jasper reasoned. "It won't be too strange for me to go into the city to my family's shop."

"We also need to stock up on a week's worth of food for three people," Ezekiel said. "And weapons for myself and you at least, I know Jasper hasn't trained with them at all."

"Right," though Nadia wasn't sure how helpful she would be when it came to fighting, she could at least try. "We- we can store things here, or if you two know anywhere that maids don't frequent as much? I usually do my own basic cleaning, they only come in here to deliver laundry or deep clean every so often."

"The barracks are busy, I'm not sure there's anywhere I can really hide supplies," Ezekiel admitted. "So if you don't mind keeping things here until we leave, that sounds like a good idea. When do you want to leave?"

"As- as soon as possible, really."

He didn't seem surprised, and he had that same knowing nod that made Nadia's stomach twist. *Was this a trick, or a trap? But no- Jasper trusted him. She trusted Jasper. She had to try this.*

"Then we better get to it then," the soldier huffed. "Can you go into town tomorrow, J? I can worry about my own bedroll and sword, that's not suspect to have in the barracks. What do you have, Pri- Nadia?"

"Well, I only ever use practice weapons," Nadia said. "None of my own, despite requests of one, and a bedroll has never been needed. If I could get them, I'd keep them here. But as of right now…"

"I can get those, at some point." Ezekiel sighed. "Leave your door unlocked, and a chest empty for me to put it in throughout the day tomorrow or the next. And I'll put you in charge of food - dried stuff, like meat and bread travels better. Get as much as you can from the kitchens over the next two days, and then we'll see where we're at. What kind of sword do you train with?"

"A shortsword, currently, I'll warn you I'm not very good," Nadia explained. "I'm actually pretty miserable at all of it, but I'm not completely *useless*..."

"Shortsword, huh?" Ezekiel frowned thoughtfully, staring at her, and Nadia couldn't help but feel like he knew something that even *she* didn't. But he nodded the moment after that, and maybe she'd imagined the look completely. "Alright, I'll get one of those and a bedroll for you when I can, and some basic armor for both of you to be safe. Just leave space somewhere and I'll take care of it."

"I can do that, I have more space than I could ever really fill," Nadia admitted, glancing around her room. "The chest at the end of the bed I can empty, just put everything in there."

"Sounds like a plan. Now, here's where I'll need you more than you'll need me, Prince- Nadia, I mean."

"What is it?" Nadia tilted her head, and Ezekiel gestured around them.

"Of the three of us, you've lived your entire life in the castle. If anyone knew of the best way to leave undetected, it would be you - even if you've never utilized it."

That's right, she'd forgotten that even Jasper had only lived here since he began his apprenticeship, not ever since he learned to walk. There were definitely side passages and servants' halls that would be easier to slip through than the main entrance, and Nadia used those more often than not in the first place. She knew the routes every guard took, and the places every maid frequented, and she knew how to avoid them if she wanted to.

"We- we wouldn't all want to move together." She said,

thinking over the pathways as best she could. "You'd get out unseen easiest, Ezekiel. Jasper, I've shown you a few doorways near the library or the scholar's quarters, but I can show you again. And I can get out from just about anywhere... depends on what time of day."

"Late at night or early morning, I think." Jasper started to roll up the map again, as the conversation fell away from their route to Stonewell.

"Then we should meet on the eastern side of the wall, there's a gardener's exit there that both Jasper and I can access from the paths I know. Ezekiel, you could go through the inside or you could go out from the barracks and then around the wall, but either way, I think that's our best bet."

"Alright," Ezekiel stepped back and nodded. "You're positive about this, Nadia? There's nothing else we need to discuss?"

What did he think he knew?

"I'm positive."

* * *

So, Nadia found herself sneaking provisions into the chest in her room over the next four days of turbulent sleep. Struggling to stay out of Matthew's way during training, trying to stay awake as she worked on studying economics, and smuggling supplies for her escape under every maid and butler's nose. She was *exhausted*.

Now, though, a bag was slung over one shoulder and she wore unfamiliar commoners clothes instead of her usual ones, pacing swiftly through passageways only used by servants during the *day* - all the night workers stayed in other halls, in more commonly used areas of the castle. It was eerie, though, she usually let herself run into people more often when she was out at night. Or maybe it was knowing what she was about to do, and how much she was putting at risk.

It was as oddly quiet as it always was, being awake so late at night, and Nadia couldn't say the darkness didn't spook her as she paced down toward their chosen meeting place. It wasn't the first time she'd been wandering the castle so late - but it was the first time she truly wanted to be undetected, and something about that made everything more stressful.

As if some obscure god of luck finally decided to favor her, Nadia didn't see or hear anyone until she slipped out of the old door there to hear Jasper and Ezekiel's whispers from the dark shadow of the castle wall.

It was cold. She could tell that even through the cloak she was wearing, but that could only be expected with how late in the autumn it had gotten.

"There you are," Ezekiel emerged from the shadows into the moonlight, equally as bundled in a cloak and scarf. "Anyone see you?"

"No, not that I know of. Everyone's asleep right now, except us and a few guards." Nadia looked over her shoulder anyway, even though all there was behind her was a closed door and a stone wall.

"If we follow the garden's edge, it will be hard for them to see us over the lattices," Jasper pointed out toward them. "And then we reach the river and the trees, so that's our best bet as far as I can see... what do you think, Ez?"

"I think this is the best spot for us to leave from," Ezekiel agreed. "I want to get a few miles through the forest before sunrise, today will be a long one but we can rest at noon and then sunset, and we'll be a good ways away."

"Do we have everything?" Nadia asked, biting the inside of her cheek as she glanced over the small group as best she could in the dim light. Ezekiel had his own bags and bedroll, and so did Jasper - though his seemed laden with books rather than any other supplies, and of course she had all the food and a few sets of clothes Jasper had managed to 'borrow' from his sister.

"As long as you do, yes. Jasper and I already double-checked ours," Ezekiel said. "This is the last chance to change your mind, Nadia. Are you sure you want to do this?"

"I'm sure. I *have* to do this."

"Then let's go," Ezekiel gestured forward. "I can take up the rear or go first, but we should stay close together either way."

Nadia nodded, walking as quietly as she could along the fence Jasper had pointed out, and she could feel him only a foot or so behind. There was a strange feeling in her chest, then, both some kind of excitement alongside fear.

The excitement fled, though, and fear took over her senses when torchlight came around the garden unexpectedly, and two voices of guards muttering to each other met her ears.

"*Shit.*" Ezekiel cursed, shoving her backward into the garden, and Nadia tumbled onto her elbows between trellises, which weren't the *best* cover seeing as all the vines were dead, but it was better than nothing.

"Who's out here? Show yourself." The other guard demanded, and Nadia pressed a hand over her mouth when Ezekiel stepped out, Jasper close behind.

What were they *doing*? They were going to get caught, and then she'd certainly have a closer eye on her, and the chances of ever getting out of this plot were gone.

"Ezekiel Rowe," instead of anger- there was amusement, and

the two guards laughed. "Out here meeting your little *friend* again? Didn't you say you'd be more careful?"

"It's not my fault you two are going above and beyond," Ezekiel said accusingly. "Can't a guy have any privacy, these days? We're just on a walk."

"At half past midnight?" The other scoffed. "Isn't it a little late for you, scholar?"

"Do you really want me to explain-"

"No, *no-*" the third voice laughed. "Just get back to bed by the time we make our rounds again, Rowe. You're a good soldier, I don't want to have to report you."

"Then don't."

"There's technically no rules against taking walks with a friend, even at night." Jasper piped up. "Ez isn't on shift right now, so-"

"Yeah, yeah, get back to it." The other two snickered, and Nadia would roll her eyes as well if she wasn't mere feet away from being found out. Had they really been found wandering around together at night before? "Have fun, or whatever it is you do."

"Oh, I hope you... I hope you twist your ankle." Ezekiel grumbled, but miraculously the torch started away, back around the castle on the guard's usual route.

The air was tense and still for a few long moments, but then Jasper's hand reached out, and Nadia let him pull her back up and out of the garden.

"We need to be more careful," Ezekiel murmured, still squinting after them. "Those two usually don't do such a thorough job, but I'd like to hope they just wanted to make fun of me."

"That was terrifying." Nadia almost wanted to throw up, but

she swallowed thickly, bracing herself. "We need to *go*."

"Right," Ezekiel nodded, gesturing for them to follow again, leading quickly off the side of the path into the trees. "Try to be quiet, if you can."

That had been far too close, too soon. What would King Richard even do, if he found out that Nadia was trying to run? Would he lock her up more securely, or kill her early, or what? She didn't even want to think about that, but it was all her mind could conjure up as they made their way through grass and marshes toward the other forest path, one she could hardly see in the darkness and the trees. Ezekiel took the lead once they were out of sight from the castle, and he seemed to know where they were going.

"Stick close," he murmured back to her and Jasper, taking his hand and nodding to her. "The further we get, the more the risk of bandits or wolves or something. Don't be afraid to tell me if you hear something or see something. Especially with those idiots having seen us... anything could be dangerous."

"We'll be fine," Jasper said confidently. "I don't think anything else will bother us today, at least not until the sun rises."

"Optimistic, I like it." Ezekiel chuckled. "Still keep an eye out, though."

So Nadia spent most of the next few hours staring out into the trees around them, listening to the flapping of birds' wings and the soft rustling of grass and water and twigs, the stars and gods and moon slowly moving in the sky through the tree branches overhead.

It was more tedious than she'd thought, and maybe that was due to inexperience, but walking along the path grew dull as the sun rose and the stars disappeared and Jasper started to mumble to himself about something or other, though it was too quiet for Nadia to really hear.

"We can break soon," Ezekiel seemed to pick up on their weariness. "There's a clearing ahead that we can stop in for... a few hours, but I want to move a lot on this first day. If we're caught now, it's..." he didn't need to finish the sentence, for them to know the danger they were in. Nadia shuddered, but did her best to focus on the best chance she had, which rested on the friends with her now.

"I wouldn't mind a short break," Nadia admitted. "How much further do you think it is?"

"Ten, fifteen minutes?" Ezekiel shrugged. "We have a good head start, I don't think anyone will notice our absence for another hour or so, and it'll take time to put together search parties once they realize *you* specifically are gone, Nadia."

"I can re-braid your hair while we rest," Jasper suddenly suggested. "You're still wearing it in a nobleman's style, I can do it like I used to help my mother and sister do theirs."

"Really?"

"If you want me to." Jasper shrugged. "It's been a few years since I tried to braid hair, but I can remember how."

"That would be wonderful, Jasper, thank you." Nadia had always wanted to do her hair in some other way, some way that a woman might do it rather than a prince or a king. The chance had simply never arisen, seeing as she had to keep this all a secret.

"Anything we can do to make you seem less like the prince," Ezekiel agreed with a sigh. "Would probably be good. Jasper and I both know, more or less, how to be normal. But you..."

"Yeah, yeah, I'm not 'of the people.' I know." Nadia rolled her eyes. "But I can at least try. You'll get to lecture me all you like, Ezekiel, if the trip is as long as you say."

It's not as if she'd *tried* to be as aloof as she was, even if she hadn't tried to be the opposite. It had just never occurred to her, past wondering what life must be like, to go out into the city and actually meet people.

Thinking about it now, though, knowing what she did about her father's plans... Nadia figured that even if she had thought to try and leave sooner than this it would have become a reality anyway.

9

Men and Monsters

"Don't tell me you lost their trail." Matthew's voice came from only a few feet away, and Nadia lay in the mud, hidden beneath a thrown-together cover of bushes and branches, and barely dared to breathe. "Did you even have it in the first place? Useless, all of you!"

"The swamps are notoriously-"

"That idiot doesn't know how to cover his tracks, even in the swamp," Matthew said scathingly, a tone Nadia heard all too often when she wasn't doing well training. "If the tracks are covered it means someone took the prince right from under *your* noses last night. Go back to where you last had it, restart. We're wasting daylight."

The footsteps retreated back through the mud and water they'd come from, and Ezekiel kept his arm out, over both her and Jasper's shoulders to keep them from moving for a good twenty minutes, maybe more. When he finally, slowly, lifted his head and decided it was clear, Jasper bolted upright.

"He called you an *idiot!*"

"Sh- Jasper!" Ezekiel snapped, head whipping around. "Do

you *want* to be caught and executed?"

"He called Nadia an idiot," Jasper whispered, though he was just as irate. "Can you believe that?"

"It's fine." Nadia sighed, wringing swamp water out of her hair and clothes as she followed Ezekiel up, into the densest part of the shrubbery to hide while they still moved away from the way the searchers had gone. They'd been muddy and wet already- but now after lying in the mud, Nadia's clothes and skin were caked in it. It was a gritty, slimy feeling that made the outside of her skin crawl just as much as the inside always did. "I am an idiot, sometimes."

"Who told you *that?*"

"Stay focused right now," Ezekiel whispered, but the look he was giving Nadia made her worry that he was just as curious, if less angry. "We need to lose their trail, they got way too close for comfort just now."

"You can say that again." Nadia was only thankful that she hadn't eaten much that morning, so as nauseous as she'd become, at least she hadn't thrown up and given their hiding place away. "W-we need to stay away from them, I…" She didn't want to imagine what would happen if Matthew found her.

Ezekiel and Jasper would be arrested, and probably killed. She would be *hurt* at the very least, and eventually killed herself if her father still went through with the plan to murder her. She'd probably be hurt before they even got back to the castle- Matthew seemed to find joy in hurting her when she disappointed him enough, and that was something she would *love* to leave behind.

"We will." Ezekiel peered through the branches grimly. "It's more dangerous, but we can go further from the road. I'm surprised they even searched this one, it's just a hunting path."

"Dangerous how?" Nadia asked, following his gaze even though she didn't have the right angle to look out of their hiding place. All she saw were the purplish-brown leaves, shifting with the breeze and their small movements.

"Animals, and sinkholes." Ezekiel sighed. "And poisonous plants, and... you know, I think just those three."

"And will o' wisps," Jasper added, at which Ezekiel rolled his eyes. "What, have you never seen one?"

"They're fireflies, J, they're bugs," Ezekiel said.

Nadia was pretty sure that the description of will o' wisps in legends wasn't even close to fireflies, but Ezekiel was the one who had actually been out in these swamps before.

"Even if they are just bugs," She said. "We still shouldn't just follow them through the trees- there's sinkholes? That could still be dangerous."

"Exactly." Ezekiel pointed at her. "Not fairies, Jasper, sinkholes."

"You say that as if you know for certain that will o wisps aren't real." Jasper frowned indignantly. "We're literally on our way to find *magic*."

"Okay, fine, that's a good point. Still doesn't change that we shouldn't follow them." Ezekiel paused, holding up a finger to his mouth as he squinted back toward the road. "We need to move. Follow me- *quietly*."

He crept off into the brush, one hand on the pommel of his sword and the other one hanging slightly back, reaching out for Jasper who took it briefly, and Nadia followed after them keeping an eye on the ground, anxious at the idea of simply sinking into the dirt.

She was sure the sinkholes he mentioned were more in the

muddy sections of the swamp, and not the drier land they were on right now, but knowing about it made the concern feel a lot more real. It was honestly embarrassing how much of this she hadn't thought about until she was shin-deep in mud and water, waving bugs out of her face.

Ezekiel seemed as confident as he could in the situation, though, and led them around mud pits and marshes and through the roots of massive trees. Mostly headed east, but the winding route they took was probably his way of trying to make sure Matthew and his men weren't able to trail them further.

"You've- you've gone this way before, right?" Nadia asked once they were a good distance into the swamps. "You know where we're going?"

"I know if we go east for long enough, we'll run into another path." Ezekiel sighed. "I've only ever used the paths, it's bad luck to leave them. But we don't have a choice right now, so... I'm just cutting through to the next one I know of."

"Oh." That hardly seemed like a good idea, but she knew taking any path right now - even a rarely used one - would probably get them found.

"We'll be okay," Jasper said bracingly. "Worst case scenario is us getting sucked into the mud and dying. As long as that doesn't happen, we're good!"

"Great."

"He's technically right," Ezekiel muttered, scowling as he shoved into a thick bit of brush and reeds. "Be careful here- there's hidden water. We should probably go around instead of through."

"Around... how far?" Nadia glanced at the thicket and then up and down it, where the edges of the hidden waterway disappeared into the trees and fog.

"As far as we have to, unless you can fly. I wouldn't trust the banks or the bottom of that creek with anything worth more than a copper piece." Ezekiel picked up a stick and stabbed it into the dirt in front of them- and it crumbled away, splashing into the water that was still shrouded under branches and leaves. "See?"

"Lead the way then," Nadia sighed, turning to follow him when he decided on a direction and started forward again. "You believe in bad luck but not in will o 'wisps?"

"For- I never said I don't *believe* in will o' wisps." Ezekiel sighed irritably. "I just don't think they're as dangerous as people make them out to be. They can't force you to follow them, you know?"

"That's why they tempt you," Jasper said, wiggling his fingers to emphasize his point. "They lure you into the darkness and the cursed places and then you die, lost in shadows *forever.*"

"They're fireflies," Ezekiel said as if that didn't contradict everything he'd just said. Nadia raised an eyebrow, and he groaned. "I mean they're harmless, so much that they're the *same* as fireflies. Everyone who lives out here has seen them, I'm just not afraid of them."

"You've seen them?"

"I grew up out here, yes." Ezekiel sighed. "Not in the swamps, exactly, but there are some forests on the other side of the lake where you could find a few wisps at night. And they're just part of the forest, the same way fireflies are. You two will probably see them while we're walking through, just remember not to wander aimlessly after them."

"You saw wisps!" Jasper's face lit up in the dim light of the swamp, and Nadia chuckled. "What did they look like? When did you see them? Why-"

"You've read all about them, haven't you?" Ezekiel asked. "Nothing I could say will give you any more information, you have a great memory."

"I've read basically everything in the royal library, but there are so many different stories about wisps that it's hard to tell which ones are real and which ones are made up," Jasper said excitedly, struggling to keep his voice in the whispers they'd been using. "First-hand accounts are the best, but even those after years can be turned into fairy tales instead of real stories."

"Right, right..." Ezekiel nodded, though something off in the trees distracted him, and his footsteps stalled. Nadia frowned, looking in the same direction, though Jasper didn't seem to notice.

The air was quieter than it had been a few minutes ago, with fewer bird calls and rustling in the bushes around them. Unease crawled up her spine, and thoughts of sinkholes and will o' wisps and Matthew's soldiers crept into her brain, bringing goosebumps rising along her arms. Or maybe they were just from her wet clothes.

"Some people say we might as well just take it for what it is, and put our faith in the historians of the past," he continued. "But I think we should at least scrutinize tales a small bit, especially if-"

"J-"

"-they don't line up with other accounts of the exact same time or topic, because that would mean *someone* was wrong, or even an outright liar. So,"

"J! Shush," Ezekiel reached to put a hand over Jasper's mouth, making him blink in surprise, looking terribly offended. "Do you hear that?"

"Hear what?" Nadia asked, unease prickling up the back of her neck.

"I thought something was moving in there," Ezekiel muttered as Jasper slapped his hand away. "Be quiet for a second, will you? Just- I just want to be sure."

"I don't see anything," Nadia shook her head, squinting through the various scrubby bushes and trees. It all just seemed to be moss and mud and water. "Are you positive you-"

"*Move.*"

One moment Nadia was standing near the back of their group, the next she was being shoved into Jasper and forward a yard or so, while Ezekiel grappled with *something*- what in the star's name *was that*?

Some kind of massive beast had latched its jaws onto Ezekiel's arm when he pushed them out of the way. It had shot up from the water, splashing all of them with sludge and mud, and Nadia could see the massive teeth cutting into him in an instant while he was still scrambling for the sword at his belt with the one still left.

She reached for her own, but her hands fumbled in uncertainty, and Nadia wasn't even sure where to start with something like this creature.

The thing was absolutely *massive*, and it snarled cruelly as it dragged Ezekiel further into the swamp, it smelled like something half-dead or rotting. Or maybe that was just the smell of the decaying plants stuck in its matted fur.

"Ezekiel- *oh stars above-*" Jasper grabbed onto Nadia's arm, fingers pressing in so tightly it hurt. "Are you okay?"

"Oh- yeah, I'm doing great." Ezekiel hissed back, kicking the beast away while the one arm fell to his side, bloody and chewed on, and he started to sink further in the mud it had dragged him to. *"Damnit."*

"That doesn't sound *true*, can I-" he didn't finish the thought, letting out a startled scream when pitch-black blood sprayed across the three of them, with one moment free Ezekiel had pulled out his sword and lunged forward, lodging it through the beasts throat and pulling back harshly. The throat now hung out of the front of it, gruesomely leaking black blood into the water and mud while the beast staggered clumsily for a few yards before collapsing.

"Help me." Ezekiel snapped, trying to pull himself out of the mud that still sucked him downward, now all the way to his waist.

Right. Focus- okay, he was okay. Nadia followed Jasper through the water to the edge of the mud pit, grabbing onto Ezekiel's uninjured arm and pulling. It took a few minutes, and she was almost afraid they'd all get pulled in and lost to the swamp forever- but then there was a sickening slurping sound and Ezekiel came free, sending them all tumbling down into the water for a moment.

His blood began to leak into it, staining the water and parts of their clothing a crimson red, even mixing with the monster's black blood in some places.

A new kind of nausea welled up in Nadia's throat and she honestly wasn't sure if she could hold this one back. She pulled away from them both, bending over a smaller bunch of shrubbery while her stomach emptied the small amount of breakfast she had eaten that morning.

"That one was uh- it was probably traveling alone." Ezekiel hissed, face pale and twisted in pain as he stood, steadying his injured arm. "At least I think so- if the rumors are right. They supposedly hibernate in winter, I'm surprised it even saw us... *ow.*"

"What *was* that?" Nadia stared down at the body, numb adrenaline slowly pulling the past few moments back through her mind. Her mouth tasted like vomit, still, and the air smelled like mud and rot and blood. "How did you do that?"

"You're hurt, oh no- I'm so *sorry!*" Jasper worried, hovering beside Ezekiel as he rifled through his bag, pulling out a roll of bandages. "What do you need? Are you okay, I-I should have done something..."

"It's not... *so* bad," Ezekiel sighed, but still leaned against a tree and let Jasper inspect the injury. "Those things are nasty but *usually* harmless. It was probably just hungry."

"What is that a- a rookam?" Jasper stammered, fitting the bandages around Ezekiel's arm while Nadia paced closer, leaving a wide berth around the dead animal. "Are you sure it was alone?"

"If there were more, we'd know by now. We'd be dead." Ezekiel shrugged with his good arm. "It's more dangerous in the spring, they have babies they want to protect. But that one looked like it was on its way to hibernate, just hadn't settled down quite yet. It's alone."

"A rookam?" Nadia frowned down at it, black fur now covered in its own, equally dark, blood. "How can you be- be sure?" They could have died... Ezekiel almost *died.* Oh, stars, she was going to be sick again.

"Some people think rookams don't even exist," Jasper noted nervously. "They're supposedly the creation of an evil caster a long time ago, which I'm not sure if I believe. I didn't mean to be loud, I-I forgot... I guess I just wasn't thinking, Ez, are you *okay?*"

That was obviously a no.

"Yep." Ezekiel pushed himself off the tree, experimentally stretching his bandaged arm, wincing in pain as he did so. "We should still keep an eye out for them, but that one at least wasn't traveling with others."

"Are you hurt anywhere else?" Jasper asked anxiously, drawing Nadia's gaze back to the soldier. "It has big claws, did it scratch you anywhere?"

"I'm *fine*, how are the two of you? It didn't get you, did it?" He was clearly *not* fine, but Nadia wasn't sure she had the stomach to pry for the truth right now. It was empty now, yes, but the last thing she wanted right now was to dry-heave or start to throw up stomach bile.

"No, you- you pushed us out of the way." Nadia cleared her throat. "Thank you, Ezekiel, I've... I've never seen anything like that before."

"Really?" Ezekiel huffed. "I suppose keeping you shut into the castle also keeps you from going on hunts with the guard or your father, doesn't it?"

"No, I- I've never..." She'd never had much interest in hunting, but she'd never been invited to do it either. If *this* is what it was like, that was probably a good thing.

"That's alright, it doesn't really matter now." He shrugged it off, taking one last look down at the dead rookam before turning back the way they'd been going. "Just keep an eye and an ear out, and we should be fine. We're almost out of the swamps, anyway, and rookams live in the water and mud."

Jasper followed unnecessarily close to Ezekiel's elbow after that, his ramblings a softer whisper that Nadia couldn't quite make out. She saw the way he held tightly to Ezekiel's hand, though, and the way Ezekiel leaned on his wiry shoulder just enough to have some support while he walked.

She trailed behind them to give at least a bit of space, and Ezekiel led them around a thicket of trees to a place where the grass dipped into a steep decline, and the swamp collected in a stinking pit of a pond- but on the other side, the trees stood from regular ground, and the bushes were more like the ones she'd expect in a forest than a swamp. Nadia was very eager to leave the swamp - and rookams - behind. The last thing she wanted was for this to cause her friends to be hurt, they were only a day or so in and it had already happened.

It had happened, and she'd been so useless... Nadia needed to ask Ezekiel for help with her swordwork, her instincts, and her reflexes. She should have asked him before now, really, and maybe if she had she would have been able to help him today.

All of the dark, creepy legends suddenly felt more real after seeing what had just happened. The swamp had gone from peaceful to deadly in a moment, and that... oh, Nadia didn't even know what to think of that, or of her chances of coming out of this in any way other than dead.

She was sure of one thing. If Ezekiel hadn't insisted on coming on this journey, either she or Jasper or *both* of them would already be dead.

10

Kindling

There was a group of abandoned buildings on the outskirts of the village of Barcombe, and apparently that's where Ezekiel planned for them to stay to keep out of attention or the sight of any soldiers. Nadia had secretly been looking forward to sleeping in a real bed or something, but she had to admit that his plan made a lot more sense.

"Be careful until we know what's made a home here," the soldier advised, drawing his sword despite the wound already on his other arm. He'd said it was healing well, but Nadia still didn't want to get him *killed*. "Stay here, I'll check it out."

"Are you sure? I-"

"I'm sure." Ezekiel started forward without another word and Nadia frowned, feeling useless to help much at all. What if something had made a home here, and he needed help? She wouldn't even be able to save him, let alone Jasper or herself.

"It'll be fine," Jasper said confidently, peering around the group of trees they were sitting inside to hide. "I don't think there's anything here."

"I hope you're right."

"I am."

Nadia rolled her eyes, amused by the smug confidence he was able to have in the most mundane, but still important, situations. Honestly, she'd only truly seen Jasper truly unsure of himself when he was worrying about Ezekiel, which was as endearing as it was surprising in the first place.

Ezekiel returned a few minutes later, gesturing for them to follow him into the run-down building he'd chosen, and dropped his bags against one cracking wall.

"This should be fine for the night, four walls and a roof and fewer bugs and squirrels than all the other empty buildings. And it's a bit far from the village, so nobody will see us unless we cause a ruckus."

"Oh, this is perfect!" Jasper followed suit, though he actually sat down and started digging into his bags. "We still have a few hours of daylight left, I can get some writing done."

"That's a good point," Ezekiel turned to look out the large front window, which at one point probably had glass in it. "What do you think, Nadia, want to show me what you can do with that thing you've been carrying?"

"I- right now? Aren't you still hurt?" That seemed like a terrible idea.

"If you're as miserable as you claim, I don't think I need to worry." He grinned, and Nadia wasn't sure if she should be offended or amused. "We're not actually going to fight, don't worry, I don't want to be executed for killing the heir. I'm pushing my luck enough just helping you run off like this."

"Alright," Nadia dropped her bags next to Jasper and followed him outside into the overgrown alley between two of the abandoned buildings, and far out of sight from the nearby village as well as the path. "How do you want to do this?"

"Try and stab me, go from there." Ezekiel stood a few feet away, sword held only slightly upright. "My arm is hurt, but I'm still able to hold my own - if you think it'll actually hit me, pull back. And don't play dirty, this isn't a real fight."

"Got it." Nadia huffed. "I don't want to stab you any more than you want to stab me."

"No?" Whatever that meant, Ezekiel seemed amused. "Whenever you're ready, Nadia."

So she took a moment to breathe, thinking back to all the unhelpful lessons she'd gotten from Sir Matthew back in the castle. Ezekiel waited, that half of a smile still on his face, so she did all she could really do and surged forward.

His smile dropped immediately, scowling when he caught her blade and pushed her back as easily as if she was a dog jumping up on him in excitement.

"What was *that?*" Ezekiel asked incredulously. "Are you actually trying?"

Oh, great, he sounded just like Matthew always did. Nadia wasn't sure what else she needed to do, but when Ezekiel made his own go forward she was barely fast enough to block and hold him off, and not nearly strong enough to push him away the same way.

"You're messing with me," Ezekiel said, stepping back on his own and holding up a hand, sword dropped down by his side. "What are you *doing?*"

"Want to be a bit more specific?" Nadia asked irritably. "I told you I was miserable, I don't know what else you want me to try and do."

"I thought you'd done training for more than, what, a week or so?" He shook his head. "Who was training you?"

"Sir- the swordmaster, Sir Matthew?" Nadia huffed. "Who

else?"

"If *Matthew* taught you that shit, he probably just wants you dead."

Ah.

Well now- Nadia hadn't thought of that until this moment, but Ezekiel had no idea how right he was. Of *course* they wouldn't train her to properly defend herself if the plan had been to kill her for who knows how long. She'd heard him that night, eagerly planning her death right along with the king.

"Well then, how would you train me if you're so smart?" She asked instead, ignoring the damning statement. "What am I doing wrong?"

"You're trying to fight like you're big," Ezekiel said simply. "And you're not. No offense, of course, but you're *tiny* compared to most foot soldiers. If I was your captain, I'd assign you to archery or cavalry, or *maybe* as a spearman. If you really, genuinely want to work with a sword you have to know how to use it, and you clearly don't."

Nadia had never even had the option of training with a bow or a spear or a horse, it had just been assumed and expected that she'd work in swordsmanship like King Richard did.

"If a small person like you wants to work with a sword, you have to be faster than strong," Ezekiel explained, walking over to hold her sword arm up in a slightly different position than she'd had it before. "You tried to shove me around the same way I was shoving you - but that's never going to work, and you know it. You have to rely on your reflexes the way I rely on strength. Footwork is important for everyone, but you need it far more than I do."

"Oh, so *you* don't have good reflexes?" Nadia asked skeptically.

"Well, a bit of both never hurts." Ezekiel shrugged. "But with you, reflex is way more important. How long have you been training, anyway?"

"Years," Nadia bit the inside of her cheek, shaking her head. "I've- I... to be honest, Ezekiel, I don't think Matthew ever did have faith in me doing well."

"Hm." Ezekiel frowned at this, but didn't probe further. "I trained under his assistants, only had him watching me for tests and assignments. But he's well-known, and he's supposedly almost as skilled as King Richard himself."

"I know." If skilled meant violent, she'd had enough bruises over the years to prove that.

"So the only reason I can imagine you didn't get the training you needed is that you're right about that," Ezekiel's brow furrowed, and when he met her eyes Nadia felt like he'd heard something she didn't say out loud, but was probably right about anyway. "He didn't have hope for you at all, not with a shortsword. We'll get you a bow in Barcombe, see how you fare that way."

"But-"

"I'd be happier if you weren't in close-quarters combat, anyway." Ezekiel shook his head. "You can keep the sword, I can teach you some things about using it the right way, but for now don't even try. I've seen enough people get themselves killed by being stupid, and I don't want you to be one of them."

"I see..." Nadia cleared her throat, attempting at the very least to seem unfazed by the interaction, But he was looking at her that way again, like he knew something terrible, and he wasn't asking whatever real question he had. "Thank you, then."

"Of course." Ezekiel turned away, shoving his sword back

into its scabbard. "Women aren't *supposed* to use swords anyway, but archery is another story. This will work better in the long run for you if you go through with all of this."

"R-right," Nadia's stomach twisted uncomfortably, but not in the way it usually did. She understood that there were different rules for women and men, and the fact that she'd been following men's rules her entire life was part of what made her sick- usually. Some of the women's rules also felt wrong, and it was confusing. Surely, any woman could learn how to use a sword just as well as a man? Ezekiel said it so casually...

"Hey," Ezekiel interrupted her thoughts, and Nadia looked up at him in surprise. "If you have something to say, say it. You think as much as Jasper does, Nadia, but you keep it to yourself too much. Runaway or not, you're... still the heir, and still technically my superior. What is it?"

"Nothing about you specifically," Nadia winced. "Sorry. I uh- you're definitely the superior when it comes to anything with combat. Being born to a royal family doesn't make me automatically better, you know."

"Sure," Ezekiel shrugged. "Do you really care so much about using a sword? I'll train you either way, if- if that's what it is."

"No, I just-" Nadia sighed, glancing around warily, irritable only because she couldn't voice her thoughts as well as she wished she could. "It doesn't matter."

He squinted again in that same way, and it had been a few days now since he seemed to read her as clearly as he was now. Despite her failed attempts at hiding her discomfort, he just nodded and put his sword away.

"Whatever you say, Princess."

Nadia really wished she knew whatever *he* knew- but

paranoia crawled up her spine too much for her to ask.

* * *

"Bow," Ezekiel pushed the weapon into her hand, closely followed by a quiver. "Arrows. Ever trained with one before?"

"No," Nadia was almost embarrassed to admit it, despite the fact that she'd never had the *opportunity* between the strict lessons she was kept in. "I wish I had, though." They were a day or so out of Barcombe, and only a short bit away from Stonewell, but they'd stopped in the early afternoon today after finding a clearing that Ezekiel thought was good enough to hide in, as well as large enough to practice shooting in.

"Wear this," he pulled a leather guard from his pocket and reached out, showing her how to tie it around her forearm. "Or you'll get- Well, you'll hurt yourself, that's all. Just be careful."

She'd get bruises. Why had he stopped himself from saying that? Nadia swallowed the question and nodded, too nervous to pry into whatever it was Ezekiel was trying to avoid.

"Just draw it back to the side of your mouth, like this" Ezekiel demonstrated. "It'll take time to get the aim right, and even *I'm* no expert so you'll have to just try your best. A *decent* shot is better than no shot, which I'm sorry to say is what you'd have at a close-quarters fight right now."

"Right." She knew that, really, but he didn't have to say it.

"And try not to lose too many arrows while you practice." He handed the bow back, walking over to the tree they'd selected as a target. "At least try to hit the tree, but if possible-" he drew a dagger, carving a messy circle into it. "Get into here."

"Okay."

"This ring is, give or take, the side of an average human's

main body. Bigger creatures are easier to hit, and if you want to hunt small things you'd need to have better aim, but start with that." He paced back away from it and crossed his arms expectantly.

All too similar to every bad training session she'd had with Matthew- but at least this time her teacher didn't want to actually hurt her. That was a surprisingly comforting thought, so Nadia took a deep breath and ran back the instructions he'd given in her head.

She tried to focus despite her anxiety, following Ezekiel's directions only for the arrow to wiz off into the darkness of the trees, missing the target tree by almost half a foot.

"Not *bad*, try again but make sure you don't move your arm while you let go," Ezekiel called to her. "If you move like that, you lose the aim you *just* set up."

"Yeah," Jasper offered unhelpfully from his spot by the bedrolls. He was trying to get a fire started, and clearly not even listening to what he was agreeing with.

Nadia rolled her eyes, pulling another arrow onto the string and sighing. Keeping the one arm as steady as possible did help, getting the next few arrows into the tree and one was even *mildly* close to the circle carved into it, but it was nowhere near 'decent' which is apparently where the bar was.

Despite her failings, Ezekiel seemed pleased and left her to it for a few hours while the sun lowered toward the horizon behind the trees.

Nadia didn't really think she was improving, but by the time her fingers were too numb to go anymore they had a fire started, so she collected what arrows she could and joined the others.

Jasper was inspecting the healing wound on Ezekiel's arm,

muttering worries under his breath as he did so.

"Are you sure it doesn't hurt at all? What if I do this-"

"No, it- ow, okay, yes, if you *hit me* it'll hurt." Ezekiel yanked the arm away.

"I didn't *hit* you, I just poked you to see how inflamed and sore the area was," Jasper said dismissively. "And it still seems pretty sore! Oh, I wish we had ice or something.."

"I don't need ice, I just need to give it a few more days," Ezekiel said. "It already closed up way faster than I thought it would, honestly... you did a good job. If you weren't a scribe you should be a healer instead."

"I thought about it," Jasper shrugged. "And maybe I could be both, there's a lot of time in the day."

"They *have* been running out of jobs for you in the library," Nadia offered, inspecting the marks on her fingers from the string. Maybe it was like playing an instrument- eventually, she'd get callouses. "But I think that might be because my father values action rather than information, at least in the short term."

"I'm a bit old to start a new apprenticeship," Jasper said. "But I suppose I still could if I wanted to. You'd vouch for me, wouldn't you Ez?"

"Yeah, of course." Ezekiel agreed immediately, despite having been staring off into the darkness around them while they talked, while Jasper had pulled out one of his books. Nadia wasn't sure if he'd been paying attention or not, but even if he wasn't she'd expect him to agree with Jasper. *Honestly- these two.*

"What are you reading, Jasper?" Nadia asked, rolling her eyes. He was bent over a book almost hunched in half, with no desk to help save his posture.

"I'm writing," he corrected. "I want to keep a record of where we go and what we do - like you said, so the *real* you is documented somewhere."

"You're starting that already?" She could only be a bit surprised, knowing his love for accuracy in records and books.

"Of *course*, the things you do to become the ruler you'll be are as important as the things you'll do once you're the queen," Jasper said. "In a few hundred years, if I don't take thorough notes, your story could be just as over-dramatized as the tales of King Arthur."

"Well, I mean, that might not be so bad." Nadia chuckled. "I'd sound a lot more interesting if that happened."

"But it wouldn't be accurate." Jasper lifted his head, blinking at her indignantly. "As fun as stories are, accuracy is the most important thing."

"Yeah, yeah, I know." Nadia winced as her fingers scraped on the flint, but on the next try a spark flew and caught on the kindling, so it was worth it in the end. "But I'm not exactly the *real* me yet, am I?"

"You look real to me."

He had to know that's not what she meant - but then again, this was Jasper.

"I know I'm real, Jasper. I meant- I meant I don't *feel* like myself," she sighed. "I don't know how to explain it, you know that."

"I understand," Jasper really seemed to think he did. "You feel like the world exists one way, and you exist another way, and you wish they'd work together so you didn't feel strange."

"Yeah." Somehow, he'd managed to explain how Nadia felt better than Nadia really could.

"Well magic, so I've *heard*, is one way of getting the world to work *with* you." Jasper shrugged. "So we'll find you a caster, and you'll feel like yourself, and the rest of the world will see you right, too."

"That would be nice."

"It *will* be nice," he said confidently. "The fastest way to fail at something is to never believe in success."

"How inspirational."

"I think that's very smart," Ezekiel said - he'd been listening more obviously this time, so it wasn't just a blind compliment. "But it's getting late, J. You two should get to sleep, I'll wake one of you at midnight so I can get some rest before tomorrow."

"What, already?"

"The sooner we wake up, the sooner we get walking." Ezekiel shrugged. "We're still two or three days away from Stonewell, where there are warm beds and real food and more supplies for us, so I want to get there as soon as possible."

"I want to rebraid your hair the day we arrive," Jasper said unexpectedly. Nadia blinked over at him, one hand absently going up to the one he'd done a few days ago, which had become loose and tangled by the journey and sleeping on it. "People are probably looking for you, and even though nobody in Barcombe saw you, I'm sure people in Stonewell will have heard you disappeared as well."

"Oh, yeah..." Nadia suddenly felt a *lot* more exhausted.

"Just making you seem a bit less like a- a prince, I guess, I want to do what I can." Jasper shrugged. "Your family can help us stay under the radar, right Ezekiel?"

"I can *ask*, pull a favor or two." Ezekiel shrugged, tossing a bedroll over the small fire for Nadia, then handing one to Jasper. "I have a plan to try and keep us all safe, but that's still a couple of days away, let's focus on getting there in one piece."

"Care to share that plan?" Nadia asked, narrowing her eyes at him, but he just narrowed his own eyes right back.

"Not yet. I need to go in and talk to them first. We'll be fine, even if it doesn't work, I have a backup plan."

"Care to *share* the-"

"Go to sleep, Princess." Ezekiel chuckled. "You'll find out soon enough."

11

Campfire Stories

Sleeping in the freezing cold, quite frankly, sucked. But every time it woke her, Nadia had to remind herself that a premature grave would be colder, and if she stayed in the castle that's all she would get.

Eventually, she *was* nudged awake by a weary Ezekiel, and she sat up as he fed another few sticks into the fire.

"You rested enough?" he asked, softly enough that Jasper didn't stir. Nadia figured he had seen her tossing and turning all night, but nodded anyway. "Get up, stretch your legs before I go to sleep."

It did well to wake her up, and she settled down again by the fire just as Ezekiel had set up his bedroll next to Jasper and lay down on it, though he just laced his fingers behind his head and didn't seem to be ready to sleep just yet.

"How was it?" Nadia wondered, casting a wary glance around them. It was pitch dark, though, and she had no idea how Ezekiel always seemed to see something out there at night.

"Quiet." He sighed. "A- a few owls, animals of the night, critters that moved into this place since it was abandoned... but they're afraid of fire. Nothing else, nothing strange."

"Okay, good." It did little to ease her worries, but she tried not to show it as she found a stick to prod the fire with, watching sparks fly up into the night. She seemed to fail, though, because Ezekiel propped himself up on one elbow to look at her. "Aren't you supposed to be asleep? You need rest, you're injured and I'm not good at defending us and-"

"Why *do* you worry so much, anyway?" Ezekiel asked, which was quite frankly not the topic of conversation Nadia would expect to have at all, let alone right now. "You were raised as a prince, you have everything you need in the castle, dozens of people waiting on your every need. Most- well, forgive me, but most nobles I've crossed paths with are *overconfident* in themselves. I always assumed that was from being safe and secure in their positions and wealth, just as much as a prince would be. *You* seem to expect the worst, and that's odd."

"I *do* expect the worst." Nadia shrugged honestly. Saying that much wasn't too much of a risk, really, and there was nobody here to overhear them talking aside from the bats and owls overhead. "I don't know if I have a clear reasoning for you, though. It's just... I suppose it's just how I've always been."

"So you expect the worst, but you decide it's a good idea to leave the only place you know well, in the cold of winter, on the off chance you can find a caster out here?"

Ah, so *that's* what it was. She had been wondering when he'd ask more questions. She'd been waiting for a good time, as well, to explain the truth despite the guilt of leading them out here with no good reason. The words seemed stuck in her throat, and it occurred to Nadia then that knowing a fact and sharing it, putting it out into the world beyond her own mind, were two very different things.

If she said it, if she explained what she'd heard being plotted, that made it far more real.

"I think," she swallowed past those words. Ezekiel... as much as he seemed to dislike her at times, he had never done anything outwardly against her. He was asking, and that meant he probably already had some idea. "That being out here, honestly, is not the worst option."

"And being in the castle *would* be?"

"I didn't- I didn't say that," Nadia took in a slow breath, letting the cold air wake her up more, squinting across the fire to try and read Ezekiel's face. He sat up again, running a hand through the dirt and rocks and wiry grass around them. Once again, he looked like he'd heard words that she didn't really say in the first place.

"Forgive me, Nadia..." he spoke slowly, now, more cautiously than he had even the first time they met. "But another thing I know about nobles, about the spoiled and haughty nobles who know only confidence... they don't spend days *covered in bruises*."

"Excuse me?" How did he even know about that? It's not like he'd ever seen them, at least not as far as Nadia knew. But then- Ezekiel seemed to see a lot more than she expected of a regular foot soldier. Maybe she'd underestimated him far too much- *damn*.

"*Even* after a sparring match, *even* after training with a talented swordsman," Ezekiel said simply. "A good teacher wants you to survive, they'd teach you to defend yourself. And if you failed, they'd *stop* hitting you and walk you through it. An injury every now and then, sure, that's *going* to happen. But not as often as you had, not as often as I saw it in such a short time."

"I- I don't know what you want me to say," Nadia stammered, turning her gaze down into the fire, watching the wood crackle and burn and become embers and ash. "We already covered the fact that my swordsmanship is *lacking*."

"I think if you were trained correctly, you *could* do just fine. You have good instincts, and you're not *feeble*. That should be enough, Sir Matthew's trained hundreds of young men that turn into war heroes and he knows how to teach people to stay alive." Ezekiel said stubbornly. "That's what that conversation became, if I recall correctly."

"So what?"

"So, what's the *true* reason you suddenly wanted to leave?" Ezekiel asked. "I believe you about the- the woman thing, I believe you about yourself. But you seemed fine to *keep it* to yourself, and then one day Jasper said you were just... going to *leave*. Why?"

"You said it better than I could," Nadia rubbed her eyes. How long had Ezekiel been watching her, studying her enough to see what she thought she'd hidden from the entire world? "They want me dead."

"Matthew does?" He sat up straighter, brow furrowed.

"Among... others." Nadia sighed. She didn't want to actually say it out loud, it felt too terrifying. "But yes. Is that what you wanted to hear? I thought you were supposed to be *sleeping*."

"Why- Okay, does Jasper know?"

"Know what, that you're supposed to be asleep?" Nadia knew what he actually meant, but she didn't want to talk about this. She didn't even know *how* to talk about this, really, what was she meant to say?

"Does he know about any of *this*?" He gestured to her, though all the bruises she had when they left the castle were gone or faded enough they were invisible at this point. She had some bumps and scratches from the journey, but nothing as bad as what Matthew might have done to her.

"I don't think so." Nadia sighed. "He knows I- I mean, he knows I worry, and he knows I dread any kind of training or lessons with Matthew and other tutors. I trust Jasper more than anyone, but he's as loyal to the throne as you are and it's not like he could do anything to *change* this, so bringing it up..."

"He's loyal to *you*, Nadia, not 'the throne.'" Ezekiel chuckled. "Honestly... when he mentioned being your *friend* and talked about you so much, I wondered why I was even trying. I'm some random soldier, and you're the *prince*, and he's incredibly focused on *your* well-being."

"Well," Nadia hadn't thought of that, and she tore her gaze from the fire to look at Ezekiel's weary smile, then Jasper's sleeping face. "Whether or not I wanted to stay a *prince*... I don't really think I'm his type." She and Ezekiel couldn't be more different. "Is that why you don't like me, you think I'm your competition?"

"Picked up on *that*, huh?" He didn't seem surprised - and it's not like they'd been trying to hide it. "And- hold on, I do like you. When did I ever say that I didn't?"

"Well- you didn't *say* it," Nadia admitted. "You acted like you didn't. Was it because of that?"

"...at first, maybe, yeah," Ezekiel sighed.

"Jasper is my best friend in the world." Nadia said slowly. "And I can't really imagine life without him, but uh... I don't think I'm your competition in this."

"I've figured that out by now," Ezekiel admitted. "He'd do anything for you, though, you know that right?"

"That doesn't mean he's in love with me." Nadia shrugged. "Wouldn't matter, either way. *I'm* expected to marry an Ochean princess for politics, and then die of a mysterious illness like my mother did."

Ezekiel hummed lowly at that, and Nadia was content to sit in silence until her itch of paranoia returned.

"What about you?"

"What about *me*?" Ezekiel tilted his head. "What do you mean?"

"You swore an oath to serve my father's throne," Nadia said simply. "And now you know that the throne wants me dead."

"I..." he paused now, looking thoughtful, and it occurred in the back of her mind that making him realize such a thing could have been a very bad idea indeed. "Your name is in the oath we take, too. At least the name the world knows you by. I swore to protect King Richard, *and* the heir to the throne, and the kingdom as a whole, in any way possible. There's no-" he laughed lightly. "There's no *clause* in the oath for which side I take if those forces are against each other."

"I see."

"I guess I'm meant to rely on judgment, in situations so strange." Ezekiel sighed. "And right now, *and* when I first started to know you, my judgment says that the king and Sir Matthew have done you more harm than any of the Ocheans I'm meant to fight."

"I didn't think it was strange at all, but I suppose I only ever did training alone with him," Nadia shrugged. "I didn't think you'd noticed, either. Either way, I left before they could kill me and that's- that was my only plan, really."

"So once we find a caster, once you're... once you've become yourself," Ezekiel waved a hand vaguely. "What are you going to do?"

Oh, that was something Nadia hadn't even considered yet. Too much was happening, she was too out of her depth with all of this.

"I don't know."

* * *

Thankfully, Ezekiel didn't pursue their conversation any further when they woke in the morning, packed up, and headed off into the dark woods toward his hometown. Nadia was still thinking about it, about what he'd said of the bruises he'd somehow seen and the fact that even soldiers trained for bloody battle weren't necessarily *beaten* as a part of that.

She had never really thought much of it, finding pain a fact of life. But Ezekiel had seemed disturbed, and he had that same look on his face she'd caught dozens of times over the past couple of months, where he'd look at her with a frown and seem to see through her to the bone, to the *soul*.

How many times had she been looked at like that and not realized it? If her memory was any better, Nadia wasn't sure she'd even *want* to try and think back on it.

So it was to an unhappy train of thought that she trekked through trees full of silence and rustling sounds and dim light. Even the path was knotted with tree roots, bumpy and uneven, and Nadia had to remind herself that they were taking smaller, less used paths on *purpose*.

Jasper found the atmosphere beautiful, and Nadia couldn't say she was surprised.

"I wish we could stay, or that we could just look around it and see more," he sighed as the path wound around a particularly dense group of trees, so tightly packed Nadia wasn't sure if they were fused together or not. Either way, the trail circled it instead of winding through it, so she could only imagine it would be a tight fit at the very least. "This place is just so interesting, obviously I heard about it but seeing it is so different!"

"You think so?" Ezekiel glanced upward at the web of branches, weaving between and around each other like a man-made lattice, blocking out the sun. "Folks in Stonewell do say it's cursed, remember, what with the rookams and other legends."

"Oh, that would be even more interesting then!" Jasper paused, looking into the trees and stumbling on a root as he stopped paying attention. "Curses are one kind of magic I can't find *anything* about at all, despite the fact that they exist. Other spells or rituals have some mention in stories, but no methods of cursing are mentioned at all. In places they would be, it's just blacked out or torn from the page."

"That's not surprising, is it?" Nadia sighed. "If magic is banned out of fear, of course curses would be one of the things they focus on first and most importantly."

"I just want to *understand* it, that's all," Jasper said simply. "It's harder to be afraid of something if you fully understand it, you know."

"Not everyone sees the world the way you do, J," Ezekiel pointed out. "Though maybe they should, we might have more important things get done."

"If everyone saw the world the way I do, things would be very different." Jasper agreed. "Magic would be legal, for one, and *real* schooling would be available to more people than just scholars, monks, and nobles."

"One day, maybe," Nadia offered despite the *look* from Ezekiel it earned her, but Jasper just smiled and nodded in agreement.

Ezekiel had been surprised that Jasper didn't know the truth, and the explanation Nadia had given for it was true but... well, there was more to it than *just* not knowing if it would change his loyalties.

How was she supposed to look at her best friend in the world and explain that her own father wanted her dead? Jasper hadn't lived with his own family for years, but she knew they were still as close as they could be given the circumstances. Would he even believe her, or understand what she was saying?

Well, she knew he *would* understand it. Jasper was very good at understanding things.

Nadia just didn't know how she was supposed to *say* it. She'd only told Ezekiel because he seemed to know already, and wouldn't let the topic go. She needed to, though, because the longer she went without telling him the crueler it would be to explain the truth of their situation.

"What is Stonewell like?" Jasper asked, pausing to inspect a patch of dark purple *something*, growing on the side of a tree.

"You've researched everything to do with our entire kingdom," Ezekiel said drily, but he did grab onto Jasper's shirt and pull him away from the plant. "Why don't you tell me?"

"I've researched it, but I haven't *been* there." he insisted. "You have! We wanna know what it's *like*, right Nadia?"

"Sure." She doubted they could spend much time there, though, given the circumstances.

"Stonewell is small, much smaller than Dunatel." Ezekiel said shortly. "There are a few legends of the area, of course, but I never paid much attention to them unless they seemed plausible."

"Oh, I know about those!" Of course this is where Jasper would shine. Nadia chuckled, listening idly as she ducked under a broken branch. "Stonewell itself is named after a spring - people used to say that the water was magical, but that's just plain silly."

"Why do you say that?" Nadia asked, mostly just to hear his answer. Thank the stars for Jasper, honestly, his rambling was a comfort she couldn't do this without.

"Magic comes from living, organic sources. Not water or stone," Jasper said as if it was obvious. "People and souls and stuff like that. Or- well, at least that's what I've found with research, but it's all *pretty* unreliable."

"So how do you know it's not true?" Ezekiel asked.

"Do you think the spring in your town is magical?" Jasper asked as if that was some kind of answer. Sure enough, Ezekiel shook his head.

"I don't think the spring or the water in Stonewell is magical," he said. "I also wouldn't consider it *my* town."

"It's where you're from, where you grew up." Nadia pointed out. He just nodded, turning to scowl into the trees, sunlight streaming down onto the ground as the sun began to lower.

"Oh, and it would be fun to stay there! I want to meet all your old friends." Jasper agreed. "And I want to see the spring, just in case."

"I'm sure there's a *bit* of time for sightseeing," Nadia said, despite her honest doubts. "Even if you don't believe it's anything special."

"Just because it's not magical doesn't mean it's not special," Jasper scoffed. "The stories only started after a legend, and legends are based in truth more often than not."

"Well, what was the legend?" Ezekiel sighed. "You know you want to tell us, anyway."

"I do want to tell you! I'm glad we're on the same page," Jasper clapped his hands together. "The legend goes that before Stonewell was anything more than a tiny village, old King Arthur was wounded in a battle against a mighty beast. He stumbled his way through the forests and fields and collapsed next to the water, sprouting up out of a crevice in the rock."

"That *is* what it looks like, if you don't mind me ruining the surprise." Ezekiel offered.

"He was so exhausted and so hurt, all he could do was reach forward and cup his hands into the water for a drink," Jasper continued. "And lo and behold, his wounds healed themselves and he found he was renewed with energy. So he set up a base there and his companions reunited, and ever since then it's grown into the town it is now."

"Which, as I said, still isn't much," came the halfhearted supplement as Ezekiel kicked a fallen log deeper into the water. "That's all just legends, J. Not everything they say about that king is true, or he'd have lived ten lifetimes."

"Well that's actually one of the stories, they say he was blessed with the lifespan of a dragon," Jasper explained.

"I just assume there were multiple King Arthurs," Nadia offered. "And they all got lumped together into one legend."

"Well, sure, *maybe*. But it's more fun to think he had just a long, complicated, crazy life."

"Since when do you care about fun?" Ezekiel asked. "I thought you were all about facts and reality."

"Facts and reality *are* fun, what are you talking about?" Jasper asked. "Debating the accuracy of legends against history is one of my favorite things to do. But Nadia took the side of history, so I had to be on the side of legends this time."

"Ah, I see. So what do you *actually* think about it?" Ezekiel made a gesture with his hand to be quieter, and Nadia glanced around warily while Jasper lowered his voice, but continued to talk.

"I don't know, I wasn't alive back then." Jasper scoffed. "That's one reason why studying history is so frustrating, you never know if the records were over-dramatizing anything. They're only reliable if you trust whoever wrote them, and if you go back as far as King Arthur nobody really knows where half the stories come from. Oh- look at that!"

He stepped off the overgrown path again to bend and inspect a bush with bright purple leaves, and white berries that hung beneath them shimmering in dew.

"I think I saw a picture of these before, hold on-"

"Don't touch that," Ezekiel reached out, pulling his hand back. "That's a Thadona's Shrub, every part of it is poisonous. You probably saw it in some book as a warning to never interact with it."

"Oh- yeah, I remember that!" Jasper didn't seem to care that he'd almost poisoned himself. "Isn't that neat, Nadia?"

"Oh, sure," Nadia scoffed. "It's great, J- *why* are you excited about a deadly bush?"

"Poison doesn't always mean *deadly*."

"It does this time." Ezekiel pulled him back up away from it. "Touching it will give you a terrible rash, and if any part of it gets into your blood or mouth or eyes you're dead. So just don't touch it."

"Fine, fine," Jasper dusted off his hands and followed Ezekiel once again. "It's really pretty, though!"

"Most deadly things are." Ezekiel sighed, hefting a low-hanging branch further above the path for them to walk under it. "We'll be out of the dense forest soon, though, and they usually only grow in shade. There's a good bit of land cleared around Stonewell, and even off the main roads we'll pass a few homesteads before really getting there. This is the densest it gets until we go further east."

"Are you saying it gets *worse?*" Nadia asked incredulously.

"Well, *I've* never been there. But those are the stories." He chuckled. "Scared, Princess?"

"Yes, I feel like I've made my fear quite *obvious.*" Nadia rolled her eyes. "These woods are... creepy."

"How old do you think these trees are?" Jasper asked, pausing to run a hand over the twisted bark. "They've lived together for so long it's like... I mean, it almost looks like they've all integrated into each other. The roots, the fused branches, it's like *one* massive life force."

"That *doesn't* help."

"Doesn't it?" Jasper honestly seemed disappointed. "I thought that idea was pretty nice, actually. Imagine caring for the world around you enough to fuse into it and become *one thing* instead of a million things, that's beautiful."

"Yeah, poetic." Ezekiel was looking around them with a thoughtful, slightly confused look on his face. "You don't need to be afraid, Nadia, I already told you I have your back."

"I know." Nadia huffed, starting walking again since Jasper seemed content to stand here until he, too, fused with the forest. She knew Ezekiel probably meant more than just what it seemed, too, but she didn't want to think about that right now. "Let's just keep going."

"I guess it *is* kinda creepy, in a way," Jasper hurried after her. "After all, these trees and the land they're using must be so used to only keeping each other alive that *we're* like intruders to them."

"Thanks, J, that also doesn't help."

"I don't know what you want from me, then." Jasper sighed dramatically. "I disagree, I don't help. I agree, I also don't help."

"I-" Nadia couldn't help but laugh, despite the unease. "I don't think you *can* help, Jasper. I just need a day or two out of the woods in Stonewell, and I'll be fine."

"Or exposure therapy," Ezekiel offered unhelpfully.

"Or I could walk into the lake and drown myself, that sounds just as nice as whatever exposure therapy to this would be." Nadia gestured around at the trees, quietly rustling in the breeze above them despite the lack of many leaves left. Just their branches shifting together, due to some wind that they couldn't even feel under the cover of the woods.

At least she *hoped* it was the wind. Nadia didn't know what she would do if these trees turned out to be sentient or something.

"We're not even close to the lake." Jasper blinked over at her. "We walked mostly north for like, a week."

"I know, J."

"And even if we *were* still close to the lake," Ezekiel cleared his throat. "I think we'd all take issue with you drowning yourself, Princess."

"Oh, yeah, that too! We'd stop you."

"What a comfort the two of you are," Nadia said, stepping carefully over a group of particularly knotted roots that disrupted the trail.

"Though now that I think about it," Jasper hummed, hands winding through the strap of his bag and twisting. "I think drowning might be a nice way to die, given the options."

"Wh- Jasper, what in the name of all the stars..." Ezekiel sputtered. "What are you talking about? What *options?*"

"Oh, you know, like- like the options of ways to die?" Jasper laughed. "I'd rather drown than be stabbed or hanged or- or set on *fire.*"

"Why do you think you're going to die in some awful way like that?" Ezekiel almost sounded ill, asking that question. "Why can't you just live a long life and die of old age?"

"I'm not theorizing about my own death, I'm just *saying*... if I happen to die early, I'd want to drown."

"I take it back," Ezekiel grumbled. "If everyone saw the world how you did, humanity would be extinct."

"That's just rude, and I don't think it's true *at all.*"

"Well, you don't know everything," Ezekiel said, which between the three of them here was quite a statement, Nadia thought, seeing as Jasper knew a considerable amount more than either of them.

"I'll learn everything *eventually*, and then-" Jasper huffed, shaking his head. "Then, I dunno, then you'll *see* I guess."

"Then I'll see." Ezekiel agreed, turning slightly to look at Jasper while they walked. "And I'm sure it'll look great."

12

Welcome to Stonewell

"Here we are," Ezekiel gestured forward as they crested a hill. The trees had thinned out over the past day, thank the stars, and Nadia had felt far better walking where they could see the sky. "Stonewell, as promised."

At the moment, Stonewell was all but a cluster of buildings in the distance, appearing small enough to be hidden if she held her hand out in front of her face. The valley was a wide expanse of farms and fields around the town, the road towards it was clear, and the only real concern they'd have now was trying to be unnoticed.

She *was* fully dressed in women's clothing, including long sleeves that would hide the heir's tattoo on her forearm. Jasper had rebraided her hair only this morning, and she just had to keep a low profile and hope the disguise was enough. even Ezekiel had noted that with the different style and the different clothing, she hardly even looked like 'Prince Lewis' anymore unless he really looked for it. So, hopefully, she'd be able to keep from being discovered.

"Oh, wow!" Jasper gasped, bouncing on his feet as they stood atop the hill to look. "Are you excited?"

"For a warm bed and food? Yes, I'm over the moon about it."

"He meant are you excited to be home, Ezekiel." Nadia guessed, and Jasper nodded. "I think we're all excited for those."

"Ah." Ezekiel sighed and slowed his step so they were all walking beside each other, instead of him leading the group. "I haven't lived here for years, J, it's not exactly home anymore. Dunatel has been my home since I became a soldier and met you, you know that."

"Well yeah, but your family all lives here." Jasper reasoned, and Ezekiel chuckled.

"Most of them do."

"Will we get to meet them?" Nadia asked curiously, looking out toward the distant town once again. "How big is your family?"

"Small," Ezekiel said, then paused. Nadia couldn't help but scan their surroundings while he thought for a moment, even though most of the unease had left once they got out of the trees.

There was a new kind of unease pricking her neck, knowing they'd be in a town with far more access to news and information since the capital and the castle - and of her disappearance. Ezekiel claimed that his family in town could keep their presence quiet, and that they'd be safe, but she still hated to think what might happen if they were found out.

"Not as small as either of yours, actually, I'll have to take that back." Ezekiel finally laughed at himself, and it was true.

Nadia only had herself and King Richard - while Jasper had both parents and a sister, it was still considered a small family.

"I've got two brothers, my aunt and uncle, and some cousins," Ezekiel elaborated. "If all goes well, we'll be staying with my uncle in town. But most of the others have moved to homesteads or their own small shops, or set up closer to the lake or even to the coast."

"That doesn't sound small at all!" Jasper complained. "How many is a few?"

"Well- for *Stonewell*, it's small," Ezekiel said. "And as for the cousins, I lose count. Five or six, or something like that. Most families around here have a lot of children."

"I suppose that makes sense, with how dangerous it is out here." Jasper sighed. Which Nadia hadn't even considered, her thoughts had gone toward the larger amount of space for people to take up, not... the fact that they needed more people in case of *death*.

"That's a bit dark."

"No, no, he's right." Ezekiel shrugged. "People die out here a lot. If you want your family to get past a few generations, you have a lot of kids or you leave. That's just... how it is. That's- well, that's one reason why my brothers moved west."

"Oh." Of course Jasper was right, he almost always was. "I understand better every day why people think these forests are cursed."

"If you keep an open ear tonight at the inn," Ezekiel chuckled. "You'll understand even more."

"I thought we were staying with your uncle," Nadia said, frowning at him only to trip on a rock once she'd looked away from the path. The soldier caught her by the elbow, pulling her upright again, and just smiled.

"We are."

* * *

As it turned out, and as he could have very well *explained* instead of being cryptic, Ezekiel's uncle owned the inn in Stonewell. He brought them through alleyways and sidestreets, away from the main bustle of the town, until they arrived at the steps of the inn.

It was a beautiful town, built of dark, purplish wood and pale stones that didn't look to be sourced from any of the southern mines, but rather just from the fields around. Nadia figured the wood was from the old, gnarled trees of the forests that had been cleared out for the town and farms to even exist.

"There's the blacksmith, I thought about getting an apprenticeship there until I decided to join the war," Ezekiel said as they stood on the porch of the inn, far too exposed for Nadia's liking. They had to act casual, though, so she looked around at where he was pointing. "And there's a tailor - not as talented or fancy as your parents, J, but we'll be getting extra cloaks and socks from them before we set off again."

"Not many people are as talented as my parents at tailoring," Jasper agreed thoughtfully, and Nadia chuckled even though she knew he wasn't joking.

"Bakery, general store," Ezekiel pointed out each place of business, though a good many buildings even on the main road seemed purely residential. "And here we are- Rowe's Inn and Tavern, the best *and only* in all of Stonewell."

It was one of the bigger, sturdier buildings on the street. A few horses were already tied out front, despite it only being midday, and Nadia could hear the soft murmur of voices from inside. Jasper gave the horses a wide berth, very pointedly not looking over at them.

"Busier now that harvest is over," Ezekiel noted. "Up the road about a mile, J, you'll find that magic spring of water you told us about."

"It's *not* magic, Ez, did you even listen?" Jasper looked offended, eyes wide. "Only something alive or once-living can create and funnel magic, as far as any records at all have ever-"

"I was kidding, I'm teasing you." Ezekiel laughed, pulling Jasper into a brief hug. "Let's go drop our stuff inside, and then we can go sightseeing or rest. How's that?"

"Alright," Jasper turned to Nadia, leaning over to whisper. "It might be best if you didn't talk too much since there's nothing we can do about your voice until we find... y'know."

"Oh, right."

Most days, that wasn't something Nadia was too aware of. But most days, she wasn't trying to get people to *see* her as a woman - only Jasper and Ezekiel even knew about this and they understood it was a process even if Ezekiel was a bit... *much*, at times. He was clearly trying his best.

"Brace yourselves," Ezekiel said as he led them up the steps. Rather than elaborating, as Nadia was starting to find was a habit of his, he just pushed the door open and stepped inside.

It became obvious almost immediately, given the loud cheer from behind the bar when the bartender - an older, rotund balding man - spotted him.

"Well, would you look at that! I was starting to think you'd died in that war and they forgot to send me word," he rounded the bar and grabbed Ezekiel in a hug, and Nadia stepped back a few paces to avoid being knocked to one side.

As affectionate as she'd seen Ezekiel be with Jasper since meeting him, the soldier seemed considerably *less* pleased to be hugged by the man she assumed was his uncle.

"Hello, Uncle Marius," he pulled himself away as soon as

possible, turning back to where Nadia and Jasper stood by the door. "Nadia, Jasper, this is my uncle... As I'm sure you noticed."

"Oh, and who are these two?" Marius rested one arm on Ezekiel's shoulder - no small feat, given that Ezekiel was a head taller than him - and grinned at them. "You have *friends* now, Ezekiel? I heard war changed people, but I didn't think it would be so much!"

"I haven't changed at all." Ezekiel rolled his eyes.

"Then I suppose your letters were all lost in the mail," Marius gestured them inward, shooing a ragged, sleepy man away from the bar to free up three stools all next to each other. "Either way, it's good to see you're still around! I heard the war was getting messy, the last news came in from Dunatel."

"No news has come in recently?" Jasper asked curiously, leaning over the bar. It was made of the same twisted wood as the rest of the town, though it was polished and shining in the light from lanterns on the walls and hanging from the ceiling. "You didn't even hear about the stay of combat?"

What? But- that would mean nobody knew she was missing... How could *that* be? Had they fooled the search parties so thoroughly, that nobody thought she'd come in this direction? That felt too good to be true.

"No, no, nothing in the past few months." Marius was busying himself with putting food on three plates, even though none of them had asked. "It's not often they even send news out unless it's of the highest import. But that's what we get, for living in the East."

"We were hoping for a room for a few days," Ezekiel said. "I can-"

"On the house!" Ezekiel didn't even get the chance to offer, though Nadia already saw him reaching for his coin purse. "You know you're always welcome, Ezekiel, and any friends of yours are friends of Stonewell."

"All of Stonewell, right." Ezekiel sighed, while a room key was handed over to him attached to a thick card of wood with some kind of engraving on it. "Thank you, Uncle Marius. If you need any errands run while we're in town just let me know. We're trying to have a... *quiet* time, while we're here. Can you help with that?"

"Of course, and don't be silly. You look like you've been on the road for days now, eat this." One of the plates found its way in front of each of them, and it smelled just as delicious as anything she'd ever eaten in the castle, even if it looked a bit messier.

"How is everything here, then?" Ezekiel seemed resigned, so Nadia figured they'd be sitting here for at least a few more minutes. "The last letter of yours I received was in the spring before we set off to Rasnia."

"Oh, you know Stonewell. Always changing, but always the same. Sonya knows more of the family gossip, but she's out helping the midwife at the Stoll farm right now so we won't see her for a day or so - you won't be leaving before then, will you?"

"That depends on the weather, I suppose," Ezekiel said as if the weather had come up once in their plans for travel. Nadia disguised a laugh with a cough, earning a sideways frown from the soldier. "We're on our way further east, a bit of urgent business... staying in one place too long could get distracting."

He was speaking in his riddles again, but Marius seemed to understand them completely and nodded, glancing across hers and Jasper's faces again.

"Further *east*?" He asked. "And here I thought you just wanted to visit home! Where are you going to that's further *east*?"

"Ridgeport," Jasper piped up. "Have you heard any news from them, recently, if not Dunatel?"

"Ridgeport, let me think…" he rapped his knuckles on the bar a few times. "No… I think the last word we heard from Ridgeport was before the winter's festival. A few good weeks before it, maybe a month."

"What was it?"

"Oh, the usual trading group, you know." He nodded to Ezekiel before turning to Jasper and Nadia. "You two are from the west, aren't you? I'd recognize you if you'd come through here before, you probably know that Ridgeport doesn't trade much with the capital."

"Do they trade with Stonewell?" Jasper asked curiously, and Nadia just rested her head on one hand to listen.

"Every now and then - when they need to. We've got better farms, and they've got better furs and hunting grounds. I have a few friends up that way, at least I do if they're still breathing, and so do about half the older folk here in town." He shrugged. "All the news they had was a colder summer, and a rockslide or two on the path up to them. But like I said, that was a couple of months ago."

"Good to know about possible rockslides, either way," Ezekiel noted. "I can check in on those friends of yours if you like, since we're going that way. Return that favor for you helping us?"

"You're family, Ezekiel, you never need to repay me for helping you." Marius nodded knowingly, and it was becoming increasingly clear that Ezekiel had gotten his mannerisms from him somehow, they were as similar as they were different. "What are two city folk and my nephew going to *Ridgeport* for, anyway?" Marius wondered, but he turned away to greet another patron before Ezekiel could either lie or avoid the question. As if he didn't even really want to know, and just said it for... what, fun?

"Sorry about him," Ezekiel murmured, almost too quiet to hear within the babble of the tavern. "He really... *really* likes to talk to people. But he's good at being subtle, and he'll keep an eye out for anything strange for us."

"I like him, he seems nice!" Jasper decided.

"He *is* nice. He's also overbearing. But everyone here loves him, and he's always willing to help me out." Ezekiel said.

The tavern grew steadily noisier as the hour wore on, more and more crowded with groups of farmers and other tradesmen around the fire and tables, playing cards and drinking and just seeming to have a good time. Nobody seemed to really care about their presence in a shadowed corner, though a few people said hello to Ezekiel before moving on with their day.

Marius came back around to them every few minutes when he wasn't helping a customer, talking mostly to Ezekiel and Jasper - especially after *trying* to talk to Nadia.

"And what business does a young thing like you have traveling, anyway?" he'd asked her. Nadia didn't know what to say, even knowing she shouldn't talk and give herself away, and thankfully Jasper stepped in.

"She's mute," he lied, far easier than Nadia would have expected, knowing him. Jasper *hated* lies, he usually wanted accurate information about everything. But she was thankful for this exception, and for Ezekiel's agreement.

"We heard there are some talented healers in Ridgeport," he said easily. "I don't suppose one of your friends up there knows something about that?"

"Mute, ey?" Marius cast her a wary glance now, and Nadia figured there must be some superstition around that. "I don't know anything about all that, nephew, but your business is your own. I will suggest being careful, miss, if you plan to travel through these woods unable to call for help."

"We got *here* safely, didn't we? Don't you worry, Uncle, I can take care of my friends just fine." Ezekiel said firmly, and whether he picked up on the coldness or not, Marius let the topic drop.

Now with an excuse not to talk - and more questions to come her way if she did - Nadia was content to sit in silence and listen to the crowd of people, trying to catch onto bits of conversation where she could.

Jasper did dig into his bags and find her an empty journal and one of his pencils, so she could tell him things if she needed to, but Nadia spent most of their time in the bar drawing the people around them. Marius, Jasper, Ezekiel- other patrons, across the tavern. It had been a long time since she was able to draw, and Nadia was glad for the opportunity.

Ezekiel hadn't been lying about the number of rumors she would overhear, or the number of unfortunate circumstances blamed on a curse.

How was it that it seemed so many people of Cidon seemed unhappy, unwell, convinced their land was cursed... yet all her father seemed to want was *more* land and power? He wanted it enough to plan her assassination, and a treaty with their enemies to break the alliance they'd had with Rasnia for decades.

All that was going on, while people in their *own* land could use help. She hadn't realized how strained the eastern towns and settlements were until now - and Nadia knew she probably still didn't really understand, but it made her think of what Ezekiel had said on that first night, at the winter's festival.

He'd said how she should try to be *of the people*, how she should try to experience rather than just learn from books. King Richard had said similar things, though more in relation to politics and combat and perfection than simply understanding the lives of the citizens of their land. There was probably some middle ground, Nadia figured. She understood enough that if she ever did live to rule Cidon she would have to engage in politics in some way.

That was some distant future, one she could hardly even see for herself given their current circumstance, so she pushed the thought away and tried to focus on the present. She'd need to pay attention, anyway, if she really wanted to learn anything from being among the people.

It was with a head full of rumors and half-thought ideas that Nadia followed Ezekiel upstairs to the room his Uncle had given them, with two beds in opposite corners and a table underneath the window.

"We'll have to talk about some things in the morning," Ezekiel said, dropping his bags against the wall while Jasper collapsed into one of the straw-filled mattresses. "But we have the afternoon to look around the town if you want to, Jasper, as long as we don't draw attention to ourselves."

"I can be sneaky," Jasper said. "*You* know I can be sneaky!"

There was no honorable reason why Ezekiel's face darkened in a blush at that, and Nadia honestly wasn't sure she wanted to know.

13

Blessings

Nadia could see why stories called the spring magic - it seemed to appear out of the rock from *nowhere*, bubbling up and running down into a stream that became a river, joining with a few other small creeks that ran through Stonewell. Still, Jasper seemed skeptical of it and she figured he was more likely to be correct.

"I don't think anyone's around," Ezekiel murmured, stepping close behind her shoulder.

"Nobody'll hear us," Jasper agreed confidently, pacing a circle a few times, hands tapping against his leg. "What do you think?"

"Sure," Nadia chuckled, relieved to be able to stop 'being mute' at least for now. "So... news of- of the prince hasn't gotten here. What do you think that means?"

"I was wondering that," Jasper agreed. "It's been a couple of weeks since we left, that's *plenty* of time for an urgent rider to deliver such important news. Are you sure your uncle wasn't lying?"

"He never lies about gossip unless it's to add things, not

conceal them. And not to me, he's always honest with family." Ezekiel shook his head, brow furrowed. "I also took a look at the board in the general store, but there's no papers or decrees or wanted posters there about any of us. For whatever reason, nobody thought to look this way for us."

"Maybe they're not looking this far at all," Nadia murmured, earning a frown from Jasper and a slow sigh from Ezekiel.

"*Whatever* the reason, it's better for us. You haven't been recognized, and now we have a good reason for you to be quiet." He said. "I only worry that perhaps they are looking, but not overtly. Keep an eye out for anyone who seems to be watching us, or seems out of place here. It'll be easier to spot someone following us once we've left town, but… just keep an eye out."

Almost on instinct at this point, Nadia glanced around them. But, as Jasper had said, the banks of the stream and spring were deserted aside from the three of them. It was a bitterly cold evening, anyway, and she was honestly surprised the water still ran instead of freezing over. So they were the only people foolish enough to be out in the weather unnecessarily, and she figured it was only going to get colder from here on out as winter came on full force.

"We can pick up supplies as soon as tomorrow morning," Jasper said. "When do you think the tailor will have better winterwear for us, Ez?"

"They probably have some basic sizes on hand already," Ezekiel shrugged. "At least gloves, cloaks, and socks. All our boots are fine for now, but we can revisit that in Ridgeport."

"Did you want to wait, and see your aunt?" Nadia asked. "If we can get everything by tomorrow, we could leave tomorrow night unless you want to see her."

"I... I wouldn't mind it," Ezekiel frowned. "And another day or so's rest wouldn't hurt us, either, it's been a long journey and we're not done yet. It's another week or so to Ridgeport, and that's only if there's no snow storms or rockslide or, stars forbid, a full avalanche."

"I'd like to get to Ridgeport before there's too much snow at all," Nadia said restlessly, kicking a small stone into the water and watching it splash. "If the stories are true, getting- getting what I need will take weeks if not over a month, and we can winter there if we have to."

"A few *months* in Ridgeport?" Jasper asked incredulously. "Are you sure?" Of course- he still didn't know the true danger of going home.

"We might have no choice, depending on the weather." Ezekiel pointed out. "And if we do find a caster, I'm sure you'll want time to bother them with questions for you to put in that journal of yours, right?"

"I mean, that would be incredible," Jasper admitted. "But only if we have the time."

Nadia would need to tell him, *soon*, about the other reason they'd left so suddenly. Why they couldn't go back without some kind of safety plan - and why they may not be returning at all. But that could wait a bit longer until she knew what to say. Maybe she could ask Ezekiel for help, he was better with words than she would ever be.

"We can wait another day, let you see your family a bit longer," Nadia said, and Ezekiel nodded. "I wouldn't mind more rest, and I'm not eager to go back into those woods, either."

"And you wanted to visit a shrine to Andon, didn't you?" Jasper asked. "I don't know if they have one in Ridgeport, but they probably do here."

"What, the god of birth?" Ezekiel asked. "Why?"

"Jasper thinks that I should take it up with him that I wasn't born how I'd like," Nadia chuckled. "I'm not so sure, it's not like he can change it now."

"No, I think since you're on a journey of *rebirth* it would be a good idea to ask for his blessing," Jasper said. "I'd also suggest a prayer to Kaphine, but there aren't any shrines for her since magic is illegal."

"I guess if we have time, I can spare Andon a visit." Nadia shrugged. "I didn't know you were so religious, J."

"I don't actively *worship*, but the fact is that there's evidence and records of the gods helping those who respect them." Jasper shrugged. "Anything can help right now, right?"

"Might as well throw in a prayer to the sky, land, and god of travelers as well," Ezekiel suggested. "You two can go on a little tour of shrines around the town. I'll give you a heads up, all the shrines are in one place, at the church. It'll be a short tour."

"If you think it'll help, we can do it." Nadia sighed, and Jasper smiled. "But only because we're friends, and you're smarter than me."

"I don't know why you *ever* argue with me, knowing that."

"Neither do I, J, neither do I."

* * *

It was the next afternoon that she and Jasper found the churchyard, walled with stone and lined with shrines every few feet - one to almost every major and minor god Nadia knew of. Her fingers stung from a morning of practicing archery with Ezekiel in a nearly empty alley behind the tavern, but she'd hit the target more often than not, even if she didn't hit the correct mark on it very often.

Nadia found it considerably easier to train with Ezekiel than she ever had with Matthew. He'd walk her through her mistakes before explaining how to prevent them, and he was far more patient than the swordmaster had ever been. She knew that was probably in part due to Sir Matthew wanting her dead and helping plan the assassination, but it was still strange to actually be able to learn some form of self-defense besides running.

Then Ezekiel's aunt Sonya had returned to town around noon, and he was spending the afternoon with family while Nadia and Jasper went to leave offerings for the gods who might help them.

"Tomera, Elbris, Andon, and then Ezros." Jasper listed off, though he walked immediately toward the shrine with carvings of clouds and stars most prominent. Nadia assumed to go in order of his words, asking the sky for fair weather and the land for steady steps, then Andon for her own wishes, and Ezros last only because he was a minor god, rather than major.

He murmured a prayer, and Nadia could only lay down the offerings of food they'd prepared this morning. The churchyard wasn't as deserted as the spring had been, with one or two priests near the church and other people passing through and standing at other shrines. So she couldn't speak, since they'd lied and said she was mute, but she could at least help in some way.

When it came to Andon's shrine, though, Jasper hung back and just nodded her forward, so Nadia knelt by the offering plate and left the small meal, not sure what else to do.

She could think of her desires and questions all she wanted, but speaking right now would only give her away and put them all in danger.

Even if she did speak, what would some god of birth even do? Changing what she was would take magic, and magic required a caster. There was no caster in Stonewell, and Ridgeport was still a week away.

So she knelt in silence, brewing over what she wished her birth had been.

Who would she even be now, if she'd been born a woman? Would her mother still be dead, or had it truly been a tragedy and not what Nadia now suspected was a plot to get rid of her? If there had been no male heir, how would Nadia have grown up?

She may already have been married off, to get a king in line for after Richard. That was his plan for her even though she *hadn't* been born a woman, and it was more common to marry off a daughter than a son, anyway.

Would she still be friends with Jasper, and have met Ezekiel? Would she still enjoy history even though reading gave her a headache some days, and some facts slipped out of her mind while Jasper's held onto them like a steel trap?

Would she still be *herself*, if she hadn't been born the way she had been?

The air was cold, cutting through the thick cloak and gloves she'd gotten the day before like a knife. The ground was hard, frozen underneath her where she knelt. The shrine was stone, as it had been since she first entered the churchyard, and the food she'd left there sat in its bundle the way she'd prepared it with Jasper this morning.

Nadia was... Nadia.

She was *Prince Lewis*, to most of the world, and she'd been born and raised in the way she was... and now she was here, and now she was Nadia.

She was going to get another headache if she kept thinking about all the possibilities of this.

So she stood abruptly, dusting dirt and small snowflakes off herself as she went to rejoin Jasper. The snow continued to fall, faintly, drifting and spinning in the air as they crossed to the smaller shrine of Ezros, the god of travelers.

A final small prayer, and a final offering left, and they made their way out of the churchyard again. The whole ordeal had only taken up a half hour or so, and it almost felt silly to have done it at all. If Jasper thought it may help, and he was right they could take all the help they could get, Nadia wasn't going to speak ill of the gods they'd just prayed to.

She could *think* it all she liked.

"I guess we're leaving for Ridgeport tomorrow," Jasper said as they arrived back at the inn, to their room where Nadia could talk reasonably freely, as long as it was quiet. "As long as Ezekiel's gotten his fill of family, but he knows how important this is to you."

"The sooner we get there the better, given the weather." Nadia glanced out the window at the cloudy sky, though the flakes were still small and few. "I hope it doesn't get worse."

"I think it should be alright, at least for a few more days," Jasper said. "It's still early in the season, but then again this is the first time I've left Dunatel."

"We'll just have to keep on trusting Ezekiel's judgment, then," Nadia reasoned. Given their recent late-night discussions, where Ezekiel prized judgment just as much as his oaths and loyalties otherwise, she didn't see a problem in trusting it.

At the very least, Ezekiel had experienced more and traveled more than either she or Jasper. That was the reason he was here with them, after all, so if he thought it was worth a shot to try to get to Ridgeport before the snow really came in Nadia had to trust that. Actually, if Jasper hadn't insisted they bring him into their planning, both of them would probably be dead to dark wolves by now.

"Thank you," She offered softly, resting her head on the window's glass.

"What for?"

"Helping me," Nadia shrugged. "Getting Ezekiel to help me. Just... everything, recently."

"You're welcome." Jasper settled onto one of the beds, journal in his lap. "To be honest, this has all been really exciting! And in Ridgeport we'll have an opportunity to learn so much if we can find a caster. Magic is one thing that I've wanted to know more about for *ages*, but it was hard to come by any information."

"Well, I'd say an actual caster *would* have plenty of information on it." Nadia chuckled. "Are you going to have space in that book, when we get there?"

"Probably," Jasper glanced down and peered at the pages left in his journal. "And I have another two, just in case. Depending on how much a caster is willing to tell me, I might just use a new one for information on magic anyway, to keep it organized."

"Ah, right."

"See, this one I've been recording our journey," Jasper explained as he held up the journal. "But if I can, I want to write a book about magic, for when you legalize it again once you're queen. So that if people want to learn, or if they have magic and want to actually use it, they have it all in one place."

That was right, she'd mentioned wanting to remove the laws

against magic once she took her father's place. Now, though, with how everything was going... Nadia wondered if she'd ever be able to put her heritage and birthright to use.

Of course, Jasper didn't know the full situation yet.

"Listen, J," Nadia turned to face him, leaning on the windowsill rather than looking out of it. Before she could even find the words, the door to their room opened and Ezekiel stepped inside, drawing Jasper's attention away as usual.

"Oh good, you two are back." He sighed heavily, lying on the end of the bed Jasper was sitting on. "How was the churchyard?"

"It was really fascinating!" Jasper set his journal to the side, and Nadia settled back against the windowsill and picked up the journal she'd been drawing in, as the conversation she was about to begin was, clearly, postponed for some other time. "In Dunatel, major gods have their own entire churches, and there are a few shrine spots within the city for the minor gods. But this place has them all in one spot, instead!"

"Yep, I told you." Ezekiel chuckled. "The people here are as religious as they come, and *everyone* is superstitious. But they just don't have the resources for a church for every single god."

"Doing it this way is more practical," Jasper agreed. "I suppose it just depends on if the gods are more practical than vain, but none of the shrines seemed to be neglected at all, even Ocheon's shrine was well-taken care of, and Stonewell isn't anywhere near the ocean!"

"We weren't there for very long," Nadia huffed, glancing over at them on the bed and starting to sketch light lines of the scene. "How could you tell?"

"I looked around while you were doing your thing," Jasper shrugged. "You took some time for that, so I took a look at all the other shrines."

Nadia hadn't even noticed if Jasper stayed or wandered while she was kneeling at Andon's shrine, so she really just had to take his word for it now.

"The churchyard wasn't empty, at least, even in the cold," she said. "So I believe it when you say the people here are religious, Ezekiel."

"Most people are," Ezekiel tilted his head back to look at her. "It's just the crown and nobles, really, who don't take at least *some* time for it. Another thing you should learn if you want to really understand."

"I-I take some time," Nadia protested halfheartedly. "We speak at- at festivals..."

"The king does, that's his job. And that's not exactly what I meant." Ezekiel laughed. "I'm not the most religious either, though I can't say I never pray or visit shrines. It just depends, I suppose, on what your situation is. The last time *I* prayed at all was before I left for Rasnia last spring."

He looked back at Jasper, then, and Nadia was left to mull over what that might mean while she drew.

Her situation right now was far different than what it had ever been, and before now according to Ezekiel, her situation had been different than it *should* be, given what she was. The *supposedly* spoiled shut-in of an heir, self-centered and haughty.

Maybe she could have used a god or two before now, with the life she'd lived, even if she never really thought to seek them out.

As a child, Julianne would teach her pre-written prayers and simple home rituals, but the habits had fallen away as she got older and tried to focus on anything but herself and how wrong she felt in the world, focus on lessons and becoming someone the king might send a second glance towards.

So, maybe she *was* a bit self-centered, after all. A shut-in literally and figuratively, and maybe *that's* what Ezekiel had meant all those weeks ago. Most of her motivations for all of her life had been on herself, she hadn't even noticed Jasper had someone special in his life until he'd told her. Sure, he could have offered up the information, but she hadn't even picked up on enough to think of asking. As much as Jasper liked to share information, he was usually good at waiting to be asked for it.

But she'd been trying, since Ezekiel had spoken so bluntly to her at the festival, to do what he said. To 'look outside herself', and pay attention to the people she was meant to rule one day.

If she lived long enough to do it, at least, Nadia wanted to do it right.

14

Superstitions

"Are you sure you want to leave, with snow on the way?" Ezekiel's aunt, Sonya, fretted over him as they prepared their bags and supplies in the main tavern room. They'd woken to cloudy skies, but seeing as no snow had started yet Ezekiel still seemed confident enough that Nadia wouldn't argue.

She was pretending to be mute, anyway, so even if she wanted to it would be difficult.

"We'll be fine, Aunty," Ezekiel assured her. "We have extra food and supplies, so even if the mountain roads are blocked we'll just come back here. If not, we'll be back in the spring or whenever we can."

"What urgent business did you say you had in Ridgeport?" She asked, turning to inspect their bags. "You only just finished training, didn't you? What war business could be in Ridgeport?"

"Nothing to worry about, the war hasn't come south *or* east if that's what you mean," Ezekiel said patiently, though the look he sent over his aunt's shoulder to Nadia made her think he wanted help.

What was she supposed to do about this? It's not like she could give any insight.

"Now, now, let him have his own business," Marius said from behind the bar. "You know the boy likes his own to stay his own."

"We appreciate the concern, really," Ezekiel said again. "But the three of us will be just fine, I swear it under every star in the sky."

"Don't take the star's name for something you can't guarantee," the woman scolded, but seemed as if she'd run out of insistent questions to ask. Instead, she turned to Nadia, much to her and Ezekiel's surprise. "Now *you* take this, it'll help keep you safe if my boy loses sight of you."

A wooden whistle was placed in Nadia's hand, and Sonya folded her fingers over it for good measure.

"You can't call for help, but that's no reason to let the darkness drag you off. Any woodsman or farmer worth their lives would go out to find a lost soul with a whistle, so long as you keep it singing."

That was... surprisingly thoughtful. Nadia bit her tongue to keep from thanking her aloud, lifting up the whistle to inspect it more.

"Just got it yesterday, when I found out where you three were headed." Sonya seemed pleased with herself. "But don't use it as an excuse to wander off, either, stay on the path as much as you can."

Nadia just nodded, holding the whistle to her chest in hopes that was enough of a thanks, and Sonya seemed satisfied enough that she moved away again, re-checking the bags they'd already checked about a dozen times.

Ezekiel looked more exasperated than she'd ever seen him, and Nadia figured the 'brace yourself' she'd gotten on the first day hadn't only been for his uncle, but his *entire* family. But they'd be on their way as soon as-

"I'm ready!" Jasper stumbled down the stairs, still trying to cram a journal back into his bag. "I don't know how it doesn't all fit *now* when it did back home."

"It's alright." Ezekiel sighed, turning to pick up his own bags. "We can go now, it's not that late in the day."

"If I knew it would be so hard to re-pack, I would have left it." Jasper continued. "Are you guys ready?"

"We have been," Ezekiel laughed, handing Nadia's bag to her as well. "Thank you for the place to say, Uncle Marius, we'll hopefully be seeing you on the way home whenever that ends up being."

"You know you're always welcome here," Marius nodded to him, then to Nadia and Jasper. "And any friend of Ezekiel is family. Stay safe out there, and turn around if you can't. No talented healer is worth dying to try and get to."

"We'll be alright." Ezekiel ushered her out the door, and as amusing as it was to see him interact with his family Nadia did so, tucking the whistle into her pocket before stepping out into the cold.

It was still morning, though not as incredibly early as they'd planned to leave, but the sun was still only just starting to rise.

"The road straight east is the best way to go," Ezekiel said. "If all goes well, we'll reach the mountains in three days, and in another two or so we'll find Ridgeport, and then... go from there, I guess."

"Alright!" Jasper seemed unphased by the shaky plan, and Nadia couldn't help but feel like their efforts to find information had been useless so far.

Everything they'd heard was either rumor or superstition, nobody had outright said they *knew* of a caster anywhere, let alone Ridgeport. Then again, Ridgeport was the most isolated town in all of Cidon. So it was probably going to be easier to learn about what was there once they were there, too.

The ground was covered in frost, not really snow, but every step seemed to crack the frozen grass in half as they made their way on the overgrown dirt road Ezekiel had gestured to.

"Are you sure we have a chance of getting there before there's snow?" She waited to ask until they were a good few minutes out of the town, passing by farms and homesteads instead as they approached the dark line of trees a few miles ahead.

"I think so." Ezekiel huffed. "Staying the winter in Stonewell is the last thing we want to do, especially if people are looking for you, Nadia. Marius turned someone away yesterday, some guy was asking around if anyone from Dunatel had turned up."

"What?" Nadia's stomach twisted. "Why didn't you *say* anything?"

"I didn't want you to start acting differently, and the inn was full anyway so he sent the guy to a boarding house a bit outside of town *and* said he hadn't heard of anything," Ezekiel said. "I didn't tell him why we wanted to keep a low profile, obviously, but he already had some kind of assumption that you were cursed and that's why we needed a specialized healer."

"Cursed?" It felt like she'd suddenly fallen ten steps behind wherever Ezekiel and Jasper were, as neither of them seemed confused. "Why did he think that?"

"The muteness," Jasper supplied. "There's a lot of superstition around that, which is what I was hoping for when I told him so."

"As much as Marius jumps to conclusions," Ezekiel sighed. "He jumped to the one that people were after you because of a curse or something, so he agreed to keep it quiet that we're from Dunatel."

"I don't like knowing that they're looking for me," Nadia murmured. "But I guess we were expecting it, weren't we?"

It was hard to forget, she'd disappeared in the middle of the night. They'd had to dodge search parties for a full week into their journey. Even if the king wanted her dead - he wanted her dead after using her as much as possible, to seal a treaty with Ochea and, by extension, destroy the treaty of three castles that had existed for generations.

"Around midday, we'll stop, and I'll try to reteach you a bit of basic swordsmanship," Ezekiel said to her worrying. "Ideally you'll still stay at a distance and use the bow, but I want you to be able to defend yourself. You too, J."

"I don't want to fight," Jasper said immediately, shaking his head. "I'll run like a coward if I have to, but I don't want to hurt anyone."

"And I don't want you to *die*." Ezekiel snapped back. "We helped the heir *run away*, they could charge us with kidnapping if they catch us. They would kill you."

"I..." Jasper sighed. "I don't want to die either, Ez. Besides, Nadia could just get them not to. She's the heir, they'd have to listen to her."

"I... don't know if they would, J," Nadia mumbled, though he just rolled his eyes. "I mean it! I- I was meaning to talk to you, actually.."

"About time," Ezekiel huffed, kicking a stone off the path, even though it was mostly overgrown anyway.

"Talk to me?" Jasper's steps slowed. "About what?"

"Why I... You know that I didn't want to leave, I didn't really want to do this." Nadia said. "And then I changed my mind."

"You said you thought about what I said, and you realized I was right." Jasper frowned. "Which makes sense, I'm usually right."

"Well, yes," Nadia couldn't help but laugh. "But there is another reason, as well. I-I overheard my father and some generals speaking, they were planning my death."

What a simple way of putting a night that still haunted her, hearing plans dropped into the air as if it had already been discussed before, as if it wasn't something horrible. It still didn't feel real, even though she'd heard it with her own two ears, and when it did feel real it made her feel sick, instead.

"Your *death*?"

"Mhm." Nadia glanced around them, but the road was deserted and Ezekiel's own head was on a swivel, hand on the pommel of his sword. "They plan to sign a- a full treaty with the Oceans, have me marry one of their princesses, and then poison me. Then the plan was to betray Rasnia and divide their land, from what I understand."

She hadn't even explained all that to Ezekiel fully, had she? Oh, well, they were both hearing it now. She hoped Jasper wasn't too angry with her, for keeping it a secret this long. That hadn't even been intentional, really, she just... hated even thinking about the truth.

"The day after I heard that, I told you I wanted to go." Nadia finished, swallowing thickly. "And here we are."

"Rasnia's troops are slim," Ezekiel said after a moment. "That's why they called on our alliance in the first place. An attack from the south on top of the attacks to their coastline would be devastating, especially because Cidon's troops know their land as well as our own, after fighting alongside them for years."

"Okay, sure, but- but they wanted to *kill you?*" Jasper shook his head. "I don't understand, Nadia, you're- you're the heir. You're his *child*, why…"

"He's never liked me, J," Nadia said simply. "I know you don't really understand that, and I'm bad at explaining it… King Richard has always prioritized strength, and I've never been strong."

"Don't try and *explain* this away," Ezekiel's voice held a surprising amount of disgust. "King or not, war or not, a father should not plan to kill their child."

That was easy for him to say, Nadia figured, seeing as he hadn't grown up being judged for every movement by the man. Even being raised by nursemaids and butlers, she'd always known that her life would be ruled by politics. So the fact it could be ended for them was as logical as it was terrifying.

"You said, Jasper," Nadia sighed. "That I can't be the ruler I want to be if I'm not the person I want to be. I can't be anything *at all* if I'm dead."

"Forget being a ruler, forget all of that." Jasper protested. "I don't want you dead because I care about you, Nadia, why didn't you *tell* me? I could've…"

"What?" Nadia laughed weakly. "Changed his mind?"

"I don't know, I could've done *something*," Jasper mumbled. "Is that why you've been so much more anxious? I-I knew something was kinda wrong, but I…"

"I've always felt like this," Nadia shrugged. "But I suppose it has been harder to ignore after hearing people plan to kill me, yeah."

"If I'm still standing, you won't die," Ezekiel said firmly. "Neither of you will."

"Is that a promise?" Nadia chuckled, wholly unprepared for the way he halted on the path, turning to stare at her.

"Yes."

* * *

The forest was just as creepy on this side, if not creepier. Nadia wasn't sure if it was the idea of someone trying to find her, or the added cold, or if the woods really were darker and quieter, but the prickle on the back of her neck was there to stay, as soon as they stepped into the tree line.

Ezekiel held true to his word, stopping them around noon and guiding her through slow, rudimentary movements with a shortsword. These she did know, but he was kinder than Matthew had ever been and he had her repeat them dozens of times over again until Nadia was sure she'd be repeating them in her sleep if she was prone to sleepwalking.

Then in the evening, when they stopped to camp, he did the same in the darkness of the forest. Even the light from a fire seemed to stop before it should, leaving only a small circle of light for them to practice in.

Jasper didn't join them, but he did spend his time pacing the perimeter of their camp and muttering to himself between scribbling in his journal. Nadia couldn't help but feel bad, he'd been far more upset by their conversation today than she'd expected.

Maybe she *should* have expected it, that's why she'd waited so long to tell him. She didn't want him to worry, she didn't know how to express the sickness in her gut when she thought of it, and she didn't want to voice it and let it be real even though she knew it was.

"Focus, princess." Ezekiel snapped her out of thoughts, and she blinked over their crossed swords. "You space out too much, you don't have enough awareness. Even when you focus on something, it cuts off your attention to everything else - that's dangerous, it makes you vulnerable."

"How am I supposed to focus on *everything* at once?"

"You're not." Ezekiel shrugged. "That's hard, almost impossible. But you can start to try, don't *focus* on any one thing until you need to, but still stay aware. You already do it while we're walking, I see you looking at everything. As soon as you start doing something specific, you get so focused on that one thing that you stop paying attention, and that's your problem here."

"It's always the same with you," Nadia scoffed. "Telling me to look outside myself, and all that."

"Purely a coincidence, this isn't as *poetic* as that was," Ezekiel said. He let his sword drop at the end of the pattern they'd been repeating for the better part of an hour, and Nadia followed suit with a sigh. "You're an artist, aren't you?"

"Well- yeah, but…"

"Drawing, if you're good at it, helps with swordsmanship." Ezekiel said, spinning his own sword idly. "You focus on details more, *and* you get better at hand-eye coordination. You have both of those skills, Princess, I can tell."

She'd heard all of that before, and she'd even told him that it wasn't like that for her, so why was Ezekiel bringing this up now?

"I've been drawing for years, and I'm still…"

"You were sabotaged, is what you were." Ezekiel said firmly.

"And so now you think you can't do it even though you *can*. Forget everything Sir Matthew ever told you, Nadia."

"That's not..." that wasn't going to be easy.

"Trust your own arms, let your instincts work more than your training. I see you start to do something *right*, and then you second guess yourself, probably because of whatever he said to you."

It was almost unnerving, how well Ezekiel seemed to read her. Nadia sighed, stepping into place again, and Ezekiel grinned at her.

Details- no, wait, instincts. Did he really believe she had good instincts? Nadia wished she could believe that, but...

"Wrong, don't think about what he said." Ezekiel burst into her worry, stepping forward with a few gentle jabs and forcing her back. "When someone's trying to kill you, you don't have time to think about your shit teacher."

"You-" Nadia laughed. "He's a *knight*, Ezekiel."

"And he was a shit teacher for you." Ezekiel shrugged. "I'm trying to kill you, Princess, what are you going to do?"

"I- hey!" She ducked, slipping backward a few steps and then around- just enough to catch his grin. "You could have cut my head off!"

"But I didn't, and now you could have stabbed me in the ribs." He stopped, reaching to guide her sword down to a weak point in his armor. "You stopped to talk to me instead."

"I-" he was right. Nadia blinked down at the sword between them, at the position she'd somehow gotten herself into. "You don't like talking to me?"

"Of course I do!" Ezekiel laughed loudly again, letting go of her sword. "But we're *training* right now. That was good, keep doing that."

"Keep doing what, almost getting decapitated by you?"

"Yeah, keep it at *almost*." Ezekiel shrugged. "I'm not Matthew, I'll stop if you're going to get hurt. You know?"

"Yeah." She... trusted that. Ezekiel had saved her life several times already, why on earth would he change up and hurt her now?

"Good!" He seemed genuinely pleased, stepping back and sheathing his sword. "Think about that, we'll train again tomorrow. Let's rest, though, we have a lot more walking to do when we wake up."

"First watch, or second?" Nadia followed him back to the fire where Jasper had finally set up the bedrolls and was scowling down at a bundle of dried meat and bread.

"I'll do first tonight," Ezekiel sat next to him, and it seemed second nature for Jasper to lean to one side onto him. "You eat and rest, I'll wake you in a few hours."

"I'll try to, at least." Nadia glanced around them at the darkness, which now that they were all grouped around the fire seemed to press in even further. "What all *do* you know about curses, J?"

"Basically nothing," Jasper admitted. "I told you, all the records about it have been erased. If there are records left, they're not available to even royal scholars. I'm hoping to be able to learn more if we find a caster, but... I mean, if they're nice they've probably never even cursed anything before."

"Well, what if someone deserved it? Maybe then they would have." Ezekiel offered. "I do worry about that, I don't want to get on their bad side if we can find them. Are you planning on revealing where we're from and who you are, Nadia?"

"I don't know." She hadn't really thought about that side of it. "That also depends on- on what we plan on doing, after. If we can't really go back to Dunatel, does it matter if we're from there?"

"If we reveal that we're from Dunatel, let alone the castle, I don't know how much they would trust us," Jasper noted. He said it so casually- it was almost chilling, Nadia had expected him to be far more upset that he couldn't go home soon. "It's how you never heard rumors or gossip before, even when you did go into town. Right? They don't want to get arrested and executed for practicing magic, so they'd not want to interact with us."

"I don't want to outright lie," Nadia said thoughtfully. "I'd like to- to try and be honest, in general, but I know that gets complicated."

"We don't have to lie, but we can be vague." Ezekiel reasoned. "That's how I talked to my uncle about you two, I said you were friends I met in the West. Easy, done. We're from the west, that could be literally anywhere compared to Ridgeport."

"I'm just worried there might not be casters in Ridgeport at all," Nadia said. "We'll be stuck there through the winter, based on the weather, and I know if we find them then that time will be well used. But…"

"Even if we don't find a caster, we have to figure some things out for your situation." Jasper pointed out. "We don't want you to be killed, and going back to Dunatel without any kind of plan would be really dangerous, right?"

"Right." Thinking about that while in the darkness of the trees was almost worse than it had been any other time. As if the shadows reached out like the Deathbringer, trying to pull her breath from her lungs. "I don't even know where to start, with that."

"We have all winter for that, either way," Ezekiel said. "You're not going to be killed, we'll figure something out."

"We could always... just not go back at all," Jasper said, frowning deeply as he looked into the fire. "At least not anytime soon."

But what about Jasper's parents, and sister? What about his career as a scholar in the royal library - what about everything Nadia was supposed to become? What about the hundreds of Ardenians who would die if Cidon went through with this betrayal plot and wiped out Rasnia? How could they just... not go home?

The idea sat in the air around them, in the crackling of warped logs in the fire, and Nadia didn't know what to say. She hadn't wanted to leave her entire life behind - but if she'd stayed in the castle, her life wouldn't be worth much once her father's plan fell into place.

There was no good option.

"I'm gonna try and sleep a bit," she said after a few minutes, finding her bedroll and settling down on it, as close to the warmth of the fire as she could get without setting on fire. "Wake me when you need to rest."

Ezekiel hummed an agreement, and Nadia settled as best as she could.

Despite the cold, Nadia found sleep far sooner than she'd expected to. Maybe because of the long trek of the day, or the murmured words of Jasper and Ezekiel talking to each other that she didn't really care to fully listen to, darkness swallowed her up before she'd even been able to try and find the stars through the canopy of the trees above them.

She wasn't sure how much later it was that she was being shaken awake, but as soon as she opened her eyes there was a finger at her lips, and it was Jasper, not Ezekiel, who knelt next to her on the ground.

Ezekiel was a few yards away, peering into the darkness, and it wasn't until she spotted him that Nadia heard what he must be investigating.

A low groan, like something dying, came from the darkness around their camp. It made Nadia's stomach twist, and by the nervous way Jasper was pulling her upright without a sound only made the fear creep further up her spine.

"What is it?" she whispered, and Jasper just shook his head. Ezekiel paced back around the camp toward them, brow furrowed and shortsword held at his side.

"I couldn't see anything, I..." he grimaced. "I'm not sure. It could just be the wind..."

"The *wind?*" When had the wind ever sounded like this?

"I don't know, I don't know what lives in these parts of the forest. I've never gone this far east," he grumbled, crouching back by the fire and feeding a log into it. "I'm just not sure if this is anything dangerous or not."

"It sounds dangerous to *me*," Nadia found her bow and quiver in the pile of bags beside the fire, even though she couldn't see anything to even try and aim at. "Do you hear it?"

"It could be- it *could* be the wind," Ezekiel didn't sound very confident in that. "It could be some weird way it goes through the trees, you know? I just... I'm not sure."

"Or it could be some kind of- of cursed creature, coming to *kill* us." Nadia tugged on the string to her bow, but with nothing to even try to shoot at she didn't know how helpful she might be.

"Well, that's a bit dramatic."

"Not really," Jasper piped up. "A *lot* of people think these woods are cursed, and that includes the creatures inside them.

In most cases, I'd say that many people probably believe something for a reason, even if they aren't completely correct."

"The reason is the darkness, and the rookams and the wisps." Ezekiel said firmly. "Those are- those are the only realistic stories I ever heard about this place. Everything else is just... I don't know, overly superstitious?"

"Does that sound like superstition to you?" Nadia asked incredulously, gesturing off into the darkness, where the groaning hadn't stopped. If anything, it got louder the more they talked to each other even though they were whispering. "*Or* the wind?"

"I..." Ezekiel sighed. "I don't know- I have no idea what that is, and it's not like either of *you* know what it is."

"It hasn't come into the light," Jasper noted. "Maybe it doesn't like fire, we just need to keep it going."

"That doesn't make me any less nervous."

"Nothing makes you less nervous, Nadia." Ezekiel huffed, turning to kick a bit of leaves into the fire, making it burst brighter for a moment. "That's your whole problem."

While he might be right, Nadia didn't think that was her only *or* biggest problem. But she had to admit that Jasper had a point as well, and all they had to be afraid of right now was a sound. She'd prefer a creature to worry about, or a person or an actual threat. At least then she'd know what was coming.

"I don't want to walk through these woods at night, it's harder to carry fire *with* us," Ezekiel murmured, turning in a slow circle to watch the edge of the firelight again. "But I don't know if I'll be able to sleep if this... *whatever* it is doesn't leave."

"Try, at the very least." Nadia tugged idly on the string of her bow again. "I got enough sleep I think, for now."

"The alternative is to just sit here all night awake and not get anything done," Jasper said, stepping in an odd, nervous pattern of steps between Nadia and Ezekiel as he looked between them. "Do you really want to do that and have to walk through tomorrow exhausted?"

"Are *you* going to sleep at all?"

The pattern of steps halted and Jasper smiled guiltily.

None of them did sleep after that, huddled by the fire with the forest groaning around them. The sound didn't stop until sunrise when the sky through the branches lightened into a dull, stormy gray. Beneath the trees, along the thin path they were following, it was still dark and shaded and Nadia felt as if she could still hear the groaning sound even after it had long passed.

She felt bad, too, for being the only one to even sleep for a few hours over the night. Ezekiel was exhausted even if he pretended the opposite, while Jasper didn't even feign being at the top of his game while they trudged out of the campsite toward the mountains, further into the shadows of the trees.

The trees that had only recently held the terrifying sounds that kept them awake in the first place.

Hopefully, it *had* just been the wind, after all.

15

Snowfall

The next two nights went just as horribly, with the creaking and groaning and whistling sounds the trees around them sent out. Nothing ever did go into a ring of firelight, as Jasper had suggested, but it was still almost impossible to get a full night's rest.

Jasper and Ezekiel managed an hour or two, and Nadia did her best to keep watch as she practiced the sword strokes Ezekiel had been coaching her on.

If anything, the sounds from the forest helped her try to focus on more than just what was in front of her, more than just the exact actions she was taking. By the morning of the third day, Nadia was almost able to listen to every terrifying howl at once while still going through the motions of a practice drill. It was almost easier trying to follow advice when she was utterly terrified than it was when she'd felt mostly comfortable.

She kept that to herself, though, as Ezekiel's mood had grown more and more sour with the less sleep he had. The same could be said for all of them, really, though Nadia found it brought her anxiety creeping closer to paranoia and it put a damper on

Jasper's restlessness, it seemed the lack of sleep was making Ezekiel taut like a string preparing to snap.

Nadia couldn't really blame him, even if the tone he took held remnants of King Richard and Sir Matthew's voices. It was uncomfortable, at the very least, but he didn't seem outwardly *aggressive*.

"Let's just get out of this damned forest," he said as he kicked dirt into the fire. "And then we can take a day to rest."

"I think it's going to start snowing today," Jasper said matter-of-factly, rubbing his eyes as he stood on the path waiting. "The clouds look heavier."

"You can hardly *see* the clouds." Ezekiel snapped, grabbing his bags and going to join him. Nadia took that to mean they were leaving, so she took her bow and followed.

She wanted to leave the forest as much as he did, with the paranoia crawling up her spine, but the idea of trudging through snowy mountains wasn't very appealing at all.

"Well, the parts I *can* see look heavier," Jasper said simply. "And I think it's going to start snowing in a few hours."

"I think the snow will just stay off the path so we can walk," Nadia said, chuckling a bit at the idea. "Just because the stars feel sorry for us."

"That doesn't make any sense."

"What about the past few weeks makes any sense?" Ezekiel sighed. "We've run off into the most dangerous part of Cidon in the hopes of finding *magic*."

"Magic is real, Ezekiel!" Jasper protested. "But I'm skeptical about the gods' ability to feel pity, that's all."

"That's where you draw the line?"

"Aren't gods basically magic?" Nadia asked. "They're meant to be in control of the world, aren't they?"

"Magic is a human being's ability to change the energy of the world," Jasper said. "But gods aren't human, they *are* the world. So it's different."

"Sure." Ezekiel paused to shove a fallen branch off the path with his foot, pushing it to wedge between two thick tree trunks. "And worship of the gods isn't *forbidden.*"

"I suppose that's true." Nadia wasn't sure what to think of that, but she knew her father cared for religion almost as little as he did any talk of magic. Past rulers had definitely put more stock into the stars, though, so it might just be a matter of perspective.

"It doesn't matter if the stars feel pity, anyway," Jasper said after a moment. "It'll take a long time to build up enough snow to bother us. We just need to be sure to find shelter tonight instead of sleeping in the open."

"You sound so confident it's going to snow," Ezekiel said. "How can you be sure?"

Nadia would have asked the same question if she hadn't asked similar ones her entire life while knowing him. And as expected, Jasper offered a tired smile and a shrug.

"I just am."

Hours later, when the path turned upward as the ground became rocky, breaking up the trees and thinning them out as boulders took their place, Jasper was proven to be right.

Snow fell through the branches in small bursts at first, but as they kept walking through the afternoon in an attempt to just get out of the cursed forest, the snow fell heavier as the branches overhead gave way to towering cliff sides and mountain peaks above them, backed by a darkened sky of clouds.

"Whoa…" Jasper, as tired as he still looked, stared up with

those usual wide eyes of his at the mountains. Even exhausted, Nadia could recognize the spark of inspiration in his gaze that he always got upon learning, and apparently *seeing*, new things. "They're huge..."

"They're *mountains*. The footstools of the gods," Ezekiel spoke for the first time in hours, but Nadia didn't miss the smile that threatened to break through his scowl. "We just couldn't see them walking up, because of the trees."

"You said two days past this point, right?" Nadia asked, reaching out one hand to catch a snowflake and watching it melt, intricate designs giving way to nothing at all as it became water in her palm.

"Give or take. Depending on how bad the weather gets, depends on the state of the road leading up to Ridgeport through the canyons." He shrugged. "The forest is cursed, and we all know it wasn't very fun... but the mountains are just as dangerous in their own way if stories are to be believed."

"We're relying on the stories being true to make this all worth it," Nadia sighed. "We'll just have to keep an eye out, and hope for the best."

"It'll be worth it even if there are no casters," Ezekiel said then, turning to frown at her. "As long as you live through the next year, and we find a way to keep you safe, that will be worth it."

"Yeah!" Jasper stood from where he'd knelt to look at a vein of bright white stone that went through a nearby boulder. "I definitely think there'll be casters, but if I *am* wrong, it's still really good that you're safe."

Right, they both knew about that. It hadn't been a real topic of discussion since the day they left Stonewell, mostly because Nadia felt sick whenever she thought about it. Obviously she knew that being royalty, there were rebels and enemies that would want her dead. But that wasn't personal, that was politics.

This... this couldn't just be politics. This was her father and her mentors, and they were the ones plotting this out and banking on her *death*. How could they be so *cold*?

"Let's keep going for a bit longer," Ezekiel said then, taking Jasper's hand as they started up the steep path. "I'm hoping to find an outcropping or a cave to camp in, but if it starts getting dark before then we can set up a tent or something."

Nadia trailed after them, sparing one last glance back into the darkness of the forest.

The shadows still seemed to reach out past the trees toward her, like the hands of death trying to take what they were owed.

She turned back around and followed the rocky trail, even though being under an open sky hadn't done much to stop the prickling feeling that rested on the back of her neck.

Jasper had started rattling off more history, some ancient battle recorded only in stone slab etchings that were now kept safely in the library back in Dunatel. Before the rule of Nadia's family line, before the original Nadia, and even before the rumors of a King Arthur ever began.

Back when people still bothered to live in and settle the Eastern mountains, before any of the wars or laws making life difficult *now* had ever been dreamed of.

Part of Nadia once again wished she was born in some different time or place. But then... if she was born in a different time or place she never would have met Jasper or Ezekiel, and they were two people she could never stand to lose.

She'd already gotten close on this journey to losing Ezekiel- and she hadn't expected to hate that idea so tremendously, but he'd become a steady anchor on her fears, recently. Nadia knew she was a bit more paranoid than he was, and he knew the forests better, so looking at him was a good way of steadying herself when the usual tactics didn't work.

He'd been hurt so early into the journey, though, and she'd still hated to see it. Maybe it was because she knew Jasper cared for him, or because she could see how much he cared for Jasper… or maybe it was because he'd shown Nadia a kind of respect she really wasn't used to.

Ezekiel had started off with all official titles, curt nods, and careful words. After the festival, though, and after he discovered her secret, Ezekiel had become warm and comforting in a way Nadia didn't even understand. He'd seen right through her, to the bruises and the fears, and he'd taken it upon himself to protect her even though it could get him killed.

Most people wouldn't do that, only Jasper who she'd known for over a decade. Ezekiel had only known her for a few months, but here they were.

She just had to keep up with her new training, keep an eye out whenever he couldn't, and try despite all her weaknesses to repay him for a fraction of his kindness.

There were only a few days until they reached safety, though. Only a few days where she had to worry this much about losing either one of them.

* * *

The snow only fell thicker as afternoon turned to evening, but soon after what must have been the sunset they did find an outcropping of a cliff, sticking out a good five feet and leaving a dry patch of rocks and dead grass.

"Thank the stars," Ezekiel sighed, kicking bigger rocks out and into the gathering snowdrifts. "We can start a fire and sleep here, there's enough space for that at the very least."

"Hopefully we can find some dry wood." Nadia stepped back onto the path to peer up the canyon path, along the edge of a river opposite the cliff they were going to camp against. There *were* a few scraggly-looking trees and shrubs, but most of them were almost buried in snow by now. It seemed that the storm had started here earlier than it did at the edge of the forest, considering how deep it had gotten as they walked.

"We can light grass and a bit of paper to dry it initially, can't we?" Jasper dropped his bags against the cliff and stretched. "I've never done it before, but it can't be *that* hard."

"I'll see what I can find," Nadia shrugged and started through the snow toward the nearest small grouping of trees and bushes. It was further ahead, so there were no footsteps to follow, but at least for now, the snow didn't go above the top of her boots.

"Be careful," Ezekiel called after her.

"It's just snow," Nadia rolled her eyes and reached to shake the branches clear of it. One of the trees turned out to be evergreen, which wouldn't do well to burn, but the bush at its base was dry and dead-looking and shielded from most of the snow, so it wasn't too difficult to break off branches and carry them back.

The other two already had bedrolls set up against the cliff face, all together instead of separately like usual.

Well, usually Jasper and Ezekiel's bedrolls *were* put as close together as possible. But Nadia's had been separate until now. She dropped the pile of branches into the dead grass in front of them, and Ezekiel glanced up and chuckled.

"We'll want to be close for warmth," he supplied at her questioning glance. "We'll still need to take watches, of course, but we might stay here longer so we can all get enough sleep."

"I can take one, too," Jasper piped up unexpectedly from where he was clearing dried grass away from a circle of stones. "You guys always split the night into two, why don't we do three so we can all sleep longer?"

"If you want to," Ezekiel sat back on his heels, frowning. "But you're not armed, I'd feel better if you knew how to use some kind of weapon."

"I can kick the fire at anything that comes near us," Jasper shrugged. "I'll go first so it's still lit. It'll be okay."

"You always sound so confident," Ezekiel sighed. "If you really want to, sure, but I agree you should go first if you plan on using the fire like that. Are you sure you don't want a dagger or something?"

"I'm sure. I wouldn't even know how to use it well anyway." Jasper finished his vague fire-circle and started piling grass and smaller sticks in the center of it. "I don't need a dagger or anything, I'll be fine."

Ezekiel sighed again, more exasperated this time, and looked at Nadia as if she would be able to change Jasper's mind. When had she ever been able to change Jasper's mind? That was an *impossible* task.

"Wake both of us up if something does happen," she sat down next to Ezekiel and started digging through the bags to find food. "Just in case the fire isn't enough."

"Alright, sure." Jasper took the flint from Ezekiel and scowled, and it took him only a bit longer than it usually did Ezekiel to get a fire started, and soon enough their tiny alcove was warmer than the world around it.

"What's our plan to find a caster in Ridgeport once we get there?" Ezekiel asked, turning his bundle of food over in his hands for a moment. "From what I know, it's not a big *city*... but I'm sure anyone who can use magic is hiding even there."

"Ridgeport, or more accurately this canyon leading up to it, historically was called 'The Path of Dragons,'" Jasper supplied through a mouthful of hardtack. "Dragons are said to live far into the mountains *even today,* that's why none of the three castles have expanded past the mountains. Cidon went the farthest, hundreds of years ago, but we've been pulling back since then after the improvement of ships and a bigger focus on sea travel."

"Dragons?" Ezekiel chuckled. "What does that have to do with what I just said?"

"I mean that Ridgeport was an important landmark, and if the mountains were still seen as a true Cidon territory, Ridgeport *would* be the seat of government. Like Dunatel in Kingsland, Caister in the Northern Forests, and Stanlow in the Southern Hills."

"So it *is* a big city," Nadia translated curiously, and Jasper shrugged. "What do you mean? Jasper..." She couldn't help but chuckle at his vagueness.

"When the crown started pulling people back, to the west and the coast, most of the settlements in the mountains were abandoned. Even more than the ones in the forests by Stonewell like we saw. But Ridgeport remains, so it's possible that the people from those settlements who enjoyed mountain life stayed and continued their family lines. Nobody really moves out of the mountains anymore, but every now and then someone moves *into* them."

"I see," Ezekiel sighed. "So it could be big, or it could be small depending on survival rates."

"And the accuracy of my research in the royal library," Jasper agreed.

"Great." Nadia laughed. "So we have no idea what we're really walking into, and we have no idea how to find a caster once we walk into it. I don't suppose the stories you had for me gave any details about that?"

She tried to think back to the scrolls Jasper had written, tucked away in her bags too deeply to bother unpacking at the moment, with details and names changed as he'd promised the ones who told him the stories - however and whenever that had happened. They'd been vague, more focusing on the joy of becoming the real version of themselves than it did any real logistics.

"Most stories said that once they got to Ridgeport, they were found by people who can help," Jasper said apologetically. "But I mean- I *assume*, at least, some casters can probably tell motivation and- and desire just by looking at a person. Right?"

"I don't know how to feel about that," Ezekiel said. "But I guess that's possible if we're talking about magic and curses and dragons."

"So, what, we just wander into Ridgeport and hope someone reaches out?" Nadia frowned. "I'm not sure either... but I guess we can also plan to ask around, if they find us they find us, and if we find them we find them."

"I wish we had something more than that," Ezekiel finally started to eat, leaning back against the stone wall behind them. "I guess it's better than nothing."

"Do you think we'll get there tomorrow, or the day after?" Nadia asked. "Two days from the forest is a bit vague, we left it this morning."

"I'd bet on the day after, if the snow keeps up," Ezekiel said. "But if we get there tomorrow evening, I'm not going to complain. Big city or not, there'll be some type of inn or boarding house and I'm looking forward to a bed."

"Oh, don't even talk about real beds right now, I might cry." Nadia groaned. The forest floor had been soft enough when they started their journey, but it had been frozen solid the last few nights on top of the awful cursed noises of the woods. She expected their current campsite to be just as bad, if not worse.

"We'll be there very soon either way, compared to the journey." Jasper pointed out, beaming through the firelight at her. "Aren't you excited?"

She was, of course she was, but honestly even the look on his face seemed to hold more excitement than she was currently able to with how tired she felt.

"I'll be more excited once I've rested, I think," she said, earning a hum of agreement from Ezekiel. "If you're taking the first watch, J, I might just go to sleep now."

"Same here," the soldier said. "But I'll stay up with you for a bit, if you like."

Ignoring as much as she could as they leaned closer to each other to talk, Nadia made do with the small space they had to lay down on the bedroll arrangement and close her eyes. It was cold, probably colder than she'd ever been in her life, but the small fire warmed at least half of her body well enough that soon she was drifting off to the wind, their whispers, and the wonderful yet terrifying idea that in a few days time she may be able to actually become *herself*.

She'd dreamt about it for so long that even now, it didn't seem real.

16

Bloodshed

Nadia woke in the early hours of the morning, when the fire was nothing but glowing embers, to Ezekiel's tired smile and a whispered explanation of the boring way the night had gone. He'd taken the second watch, apparently, so Nadia sat up and moved to the side to let him sleep close to Jasper for the next few hours until dawn, or a bit past it.

The snow had stopped, and some of the clouds had broken to reveal the stars shining brightly. Something about cold air always made stars seem so much more obvious in the sky, even when she was just looking up at them from the windowsill in her bedroom on sleepless nights.

In the cold and quiet like this, aside from Ezekiel's snoring, it wasn't hard to see why the gods were symbolized by the stars. If whoever made that decision had looked upward on a night like this, of *course* they'd been inspired.

Nadia moved around the fire to get a better view from beneath the rock outcrop they'd camped under, taking a moment to stir the coals and make them burn just a bit brighter and warmer before settling down, glancing down the path and toward the river every now and then.

The land was as quiet as the sky tonight, which was a relief after the sounds of the cursed forest that still felt like a fresh memory rather than a day-old one. They were out of the trees now, and they would be in Ridgeport until spring melted the snow and they had a plan on where to go from here.

She would be her true self then, if Jasper's hunch was right, but that wouldn't change the fact that the war their land was currently in was about to get far worse than it already was.

King Richard was planning to break the treaty of three castles. The alliance had carried Ardenia through centuries of relative peace until the time came that the Oceans had gotten in a tussle with Rasnia, and the alliance called upon Cidon to help...

Now, if her father's plan went through, Cidon wouldn't be helping them at all.

Instead of trying to stop that, instead of fighting her father on it and saving the lives of dozens if not hundreds of soldiers like Ezekiel, Nadia was out here in the mountains. She was as far as she could be from any political center or war front, all because she didn't quite feel like herself.

Well, that was dumbing it down a bit too much. Nadia had never been able to really explain the feeling of her body and name being *wrong*, but Jasper had understood it well enough and it seemed that Ezekiel had started to in the past weeks.

The night she first *really* met Ezekiel, he'd told her to look outside of herself and try to understand the people. She did have a better understanding now, at least, of some of Cidon's people after traveling through and seeing their towns and homesteads. But it was on a *selfish* mission.

Maybe she was just as bad as King Richard was.

No. If Nadia ever had children, if she lived that long, she would never plan to kill one of them. She wasn't as bad as her father, even if she was running selfishly into the mountains.

What could she possibly try to do to stop her father's armies, as well as Ochea's?

She was just one person, whether a prince or a princess or just some... person. What could she possibly do to change this?

Usurp her father for the throne, if she had any real talent in swordsmanship or archery. Ezekiel was kind, and he was certainly a better teacher than Matthew had been, but Nadia knew she was still quite miserable at both. Archery *was* a bit better, if only for the lack of painful memories associated with it.

Maybe one of the casters could make some kind of curse or poison that could take care of it for her.

That seemed stupid, and Nadia found herself more nauseous than usual at the idea of causing her own father to die. Hadn't she just promised herself she wouldn't stoop to that level, that she wasn't as bad as he was? And now here she was, wondering how she could try and kill him.

Had he felt any of the nausea she felt now, when he put *his* plans in place? When he lied to his kingdom and their allies, when he said they had a possible peace treaty that was really just her death warrant?

His calloused voice from that night crept back into Nadia's mind as she sat there, and she honestly wasn't sure if he'd felt bad about it in the slightest.

Nadia wasn't sure how to feel. Honestly, she didn't know if she felt anything at all about that fact. It just felt like a gaping hole in her chest, dwelling on it for too long under the sky and the gods.

She was getting ahead of herself. There would be no death, no usurping, if they didn't make it through the winter here in Ridgeport. That's what she should focus on, not... not all of this. Not a mess she hadn't started, even if it was her birthright to clean it up.

That could come later, like Jasper had said. Once she was the person she wanted to be, that's when Nadia could focus on becoming the ruler she wanted to be. All Nadia wanted to do was actually *get* to that point. It still weighed on her mind, knowing that people could die and she'd done nothing to help them even if she had no idea how she might do it.

The sky lightened ever so slowly, and the last of the embers died and left the air freezing around her where she sat at the edge of the snowbanks. But the cold had frozen the snow into crunched ice, rather than wet heaps, so as long as she didn't move much she could put off getting soaked.

Eventually, the sun fully came into view above the mountains, shining beams past the clouds, down through the canyon back toward the forest they came from. But even then, it was another hour or so before Jasper and Ezekiel stirred awake.

"Oh, good, we're all still alive," Ezekiel said once he'd sat up, rubbing his face with a sigh. "How was it, Princess?"

"It was quiet," Nadia said. "And aren't we supposed to be pretending not to be from Dunatel? You'll want to keep from calling me that."

He scowled, but she supposed they'd come a long way from where they started seeing as he usually did just call her Nadia. Everything had changed since they first met. He knew who she was now, he knew the truth about everything...

She was glad, really, that Jasper had convinced her to ask him for help.

"Let's move on as soon as we can." Ezekiel stood, while Jasper still grumbled as he woke. "The less time we're on the road, the better."

"What do you think, Jasper, is it going to snow again today?" Nadia dumped snow into the dead fire, then kicked apart the stones. They'd taken less care the past few days at erasing their trail, but a campsite so obvious still made her worry about being followed.

If they could get to Ridgeport just before the canyon was unwalkable, they'd be safe. If they got there and then got followed in by her father's men, what would stop them from just killing her *and* Ezekiel and Jasper here in the mountains? How much of their plans for a marriage treaty were still intact, after she'd run away?

"I dunno, maybe," Jasper sat up with a groan, squinting at the sky. "Not as much."

"You were really confident about it yesterday and you were right, so I thought it was worth asking." Nadia shrugged. "But if you don't know…"

"I'm *always* right," Jasper said indignantly, and Ezekiel chuckled from where he was packing up the bedrolls. "I said *maybe* because there are some clouds but not a full sky, it's still very cold but the air feels drier here, and weather can be unpredictable at even the best of times anyway. I-"

"I was teasing you, J, I know why you said it," Nadia assured him. "Let's hope it doesn't snow again until we get there."

"Hope is well and good," Ezekiel handed her a bag. "But we need to *go*, come on Jasper."

"Yeah, yeah, yeah," Jasper sighed and took his own bag,

surveying the now dismantled camp with a glance before turning to follow Nadia to the path, hardly visible through the snow - and only visible at all because of the lack of large bumps from boulders on it. "I want to get there just as much as you do."

"Oh, don't tell me you're tired of walking." Ezekiel scoffed. "I thought we were all having a great time, was I wrong?"

"I could walk more if I had to," Jasper took the joke seriously, as always, and Nadia smiled. "But I'm excited to see what kind of town or city Ridgeport is, and I'm excited to see what we can learn there. Shelter and a bed will be nice too, of course, and helping you, Nadia. There's a lot of reasons to be excited to get there."

"What, you think they have a library full of lost texts and scrolls?" Ezekiel asked incredulously.

"I think if anywhere in Cidon has forbidden knowledge hidden away, this would be it," Jasper said. "And even if not, I can get information from the source when we find a caster."

"He has a point," Nadia offered. "Ridgeport is basically ignored politically and historically unless you're obsessed with learning."

"You don't have to agree with him, he already thinks he knows everything," Ezekiel complained, bending down to throw a handful of snow at her. As frozen and dry as it had become, it just puffed into powder in the air in front of her face, but it did stick to her eyelashes and hair in an annoying way.

"We've talked about this," Jasper said. "I don't think I know *everything*. I just intend to, someday."

"Yeah, that's what I love about ya," Ezekiel said, shaking his head. "You could still at least try to act like you aren't a walking library."

"You're fighting a losing battle, Ezekiel," Nadia chuckled. "This is *Jasper*."

"An easy battle isn't one worth fighting," Ezekiel replied. "No matter which side you're on. And it's not *really* a fight, it's advice."

"I've taken your advice before." Jasper protested. "Especially recently. It just usually doesn't apply to me when I'm *studying*."

"Maybe you study too much."

"I've spent the last three weeks walking through a forest, Ezekiel," Jasper said. "Though to be honest, it's been incredibly interesting to be able to see the forest and the journey in person rather than just in writing from other people, so you might have a point about that whole experience thing."

"Sorry, might? I was *completely right*."

Listening to them go back and forth, as they had been for days, Nadia couldn't help but think that maybe Jasper wasn't the only one in their group to have an ego problem. Jasper was more obvious since he always just said what he was thinking, but Ezekiel clearly thought well of himself, too. Both had helped her more than she could have imagined, so perhaps they deserved the confidence.

It was probably easier for them to be confident than it was for her, seeing as she wasn't even herself yet.

* * *

The canyon was all but silent as they walked, aside from the voices of her friends and the crunching of snow beneath their feet. It was slower going than Nadia would have liked, but the further in they went the more it sloped upward - and the deeper the snowdrifts became. Sometime around noon, the path became indistinguishable from the rocks and land around it beneath the snow save for large wooden posts, ten or twelve feet, jutting out of the earth every now and then.

That was enough to follow, at least for now, so she tried not to worry so much.

That was easier said than done.

Silence had always brought too much to think about, and part of Nadia wished she had scrolls to read or lessons to do, or even some kind of training. They needed to walk as far as possible today, to make tomorrow's trek shorter, and any arrows she tried to use right now would just get lost beneath snowdrifts.

Instead, she was left to ponder their journey or listen to Jasper and Ezekiel murmuring things to each other. Either about history, or what they'd do when they finally got to a town again, or what they would have done differently about the trip if they got to redo it, all those were mixed together in the way their conversations always tangled up.

"I'd have left sooner if we could," Ezekiel said at one point, turning to help them both up a particularly steep incline. "But of course, we left as soon as possible after you were so intense about it, Nadia."

"I would have tried to pack snowshoes." Jasper brushed himself off, though it wasn't much use seeing as they were all quite damp and refrozen with snow.

"It hasn't been too bad," Nadia offered weakly, even as the wind howled through the canyon and cut through her clothes and cloak. "It only started snowing yesterday, it could have been sooner."

"That's very true, I expected more," Ezekiel admitted. "As

annoying as this is, it won't be too much of a bother since we'll probably arrive tomorrow."

"Unless it gets worse."

"It won't." Jasper squinted up at the sky. "Probably. There are more clouds now, but they don't seem as... I dunno, the air feels different here."

It was a strange statement, unusually vague for Jasper, but Nadia couldn't disagree. While the valleys and forests of Cidon were humid, even with the river that ran along the base of the canyon, the air here felt dry the higher they got. Maybe it was the increased cold, or maybe it was the lack of true lakes and marshes, but the skin on her hands and face had started to crack a bit from it.

"Even if it does start snowing again, we won't be in real trouble unless it's a blizzard." Ezekiel reasoned. "These posts will show no matter how high the snow gets."

Another gust of wind swept through, sending snow up into their faces and dancing along through the canyon back the way they'd come. It sounded strange here, louder and sadder than Nadia had ever thought the wind could get. It felt like something from a story she would read, but not something she would think was real.

"Let's keep moving." Ezekiel turned from where they'd all stopped to watch the snow swirl below them. So Nadia trudged forward, and Jasper only took a bit longer to keep pace with them.

It was closer to evening, or at least Nadia assumed it must be, when they spotted a few columns of chimney smoke over the ridge ahead of them.

"That must be Ridgeport," Ezekiel pointed them out, and they were obvious against the backdrop of cliffs even with the sun setting. "It's too far to make it today, but… but we're almost there. We can camp at the base of the ridge, and then tomorrow go around it and up."

"Oh, I can't wait." Jasper sighed. "It's so cold out here, and I just want to sleep for a whole day."

"What, you're not gonna go searching for casters the first chance you get?" Nadia asked, and he shook his head.

"Not anymore. I'll do that after we rest."

"I was gonna make you rest anyway," Ezekiel told him. "And we've still got to sleep out here with a fire for another night, don't get ahead of yourself."

"Part of me thinks Ezekiel likes being out here more than he likes a real house," Nadia said, amused by the way he rolled his eyes.

"Don't get me wrong, I want to rest just as much as you do. But you can't say the walk has been completely miserable."

"Speak for yourself, you're *used* to it," Nadia said, though she could say for a fact that she was far more used to walking all day *now* than she had been when they started their journey weeks ago. He had still trained for years for things like this, while most of her lessons had been on politics and economics.

"If you think I'll let you get back to only books over the winter, you're wrong," Ezekiel informed her as if he could hear what she was thinking. "I'm sure there's *someplace* in Ridgeport where I can get you further with your swordsmanship and archery. You too, Jasper, if you change your mind."

"I won't," Jasper said immediately. "Fighting isn't my thing."

* * *

It was cold and quiet, trudging through the snow as they

tried to reach the ridge before it got too dark. The canyon trail twisted in ways they hadn't expected, with the river meandering and making cliffs and drop-offs every now and then *that* required them to follow its path, with the only glimpse of a bridge being a few miles ahead.

Conversation fell away when they realized it was further in practice than it was in true distance, but Nadia still felt like they could get to Ridgeport by some time the next day.

It was so oddly still and silent, with the only sound being the way the frozen snow cracked as they waded through it.

The silence was broken, however, with a sudden burst of cracking footsteps, the snow surface breaking beneath a blur of pale brown fur and leathery wings that tumbled closer to the cliff's edge, taking Ezekiel right with it.

And then he *screamed*.

It bounced around the canyon, echoing and making fear crawl up Nadia's spine in an instant.

"What *is* that?" Jasper fell backward into the snow, but Nadia scrambled uselessly for the bow and the quiver at her side.

The snow around him was already scarlet with blood, and the beast on top of him didn't seem to notice or even care that she and Jasper were there. It was a far cry from the rookam - so much *bigger*, but it had also caught him off guard and it seemed so much more frenzied as another spatter of blood stained the snow red.

"No- *no*, Nadia *do* something!"

"Shit, shit-" What was she supposed to do? *Ezekiel* was supposed to be the one protecting *them*, not...

She drew an arrow, fingers stinging from the cold. She had to *try*, she had to do *something*.

The arrow hissed through the air and into the beast's

shoulder, but it only let out a strangled yowl of pain before it returned to Ezekiel, who had somehow gotten a dagger of his own into his hand and crawled back a foot in that small moment.

The wound hadn't even seemed to bother it- his arm was all but shredded, oh *stars...*

She drew another - but aiming at somewhere vulnerable felt impossible. It felt impossible to aim for the beast at all, but she'd already succeeded once...

It hit the side of its chest, and the scarlet in the snow was added to when it started to bleed sluggishly.

"What is this thing?" She demanded, pulling out another arrow as she backed up with Jasper.

"I-I don't know! Shit, *Ezekiel!*" He made to step forward, like a madman, but Nadia didn't bother to try and stop him as she drew the arrow back again.

This one *missed*.

Ezekiel screamed again, voice weaker and far more desperate.

"No, No, *stop it!*" Jasper screamed too, louder than Nadia had ever heard his voice. That wasn't what pulled the breath out of her chest, though, and made everything on the snowy cliffside come to a sudden halt.

A flash of amber light blinded her, and the snow beneath them crackled and melted and then froze again into a spike of ice, pushing the beast upward and through it, away from the soldier that lay on the ground.

Jasper's hand was outstretched, and the air around him was filled with some kind of amber light, or dust... Nadia had never seen anything like that before.

What the *hell*?

Jasper seemed frozen, his other hand reaching up to brace the one that had flown outward, and Nadia felt as frozen as the new ice around them until she heard Ezekiel groan.

Shit.

She abandoned the bow to scramble over the jagged ice, pulling her scarf off for *some* attempt of a bandage. Nadia didn't know much first aid, she only knew what she'd seen Ezekiel and Jasper do these past few weeks, but she could at least try.

His forearms had the worst of it, from where he'd tried to defend himself, and the beast's claws had torn up a good bit of his shoulder and chest as well, but his armor at least took some of the brunt of it there.

"You're okay," he rasped, looking relieved past the blood on his face, which was paler than she'd ever seen it. He seemed barely conscious, with his slurred speech and unfocused gaze. That was far too close for comfort, and Nadia had been *useless*.

"Shut up, you could've died." Nadia tugged him a bit further from the cliff edge, not truly sure how to help. "What do you need?"

"Pressure, stop the…" Ezekiel groaned again, eyes fluttering closed for a moment before he forced them open again. "…bleeding."

So she pressed a bundled hand to where most of it was from, though his arms were a mess so it might not *really* help. She needed real bandages, she needed to know more than she did.

"Hell…" he tried to sit up and winced, shaking his head as he fell back against the ground with a painful-sounding thump. "How did you do that?"

"I…" Nadia looked up to where the beast was impaled, where the spike of ice still held an amber glow. It was a creature she'd never seen before, some kind of pale brown panther - with leathery wings hanging limply from its shoulder blades. A *myth* of some kind, just as much as whatever Jasper had done was. What *had* he done? "I didn't."

"What.." he let her wrap the scarf tightly around the injured arm now, eyes darting around the scene and then back toward Jasper, who was still frozen in place. "Jasper?"

That seemed to break whatever spell he was under, and Jasper started rummaging through his bags for the real bandages as he stumbled over.

The air around him still hummed with that amber light.

What on *earth...*

"J, you're a *caster?*"

17

Trust: Broken

Of course. That was the only thing that made sense, that was the only way Jasper could have erupted in light and controlled snow and ice the way he just had.

He was a caster.

Nadia didn't know what to think. It felt the way she'd felt the night she heard the plot of her death, information drilling into her chest and making it hollow and painfully empty.

"I'm *sorry*," Jasper pressed the bandages into her hand before turning, falling to his knees to vomit into the snow that was left, that hadn't been used in whatever magic just occurred.

She turned away from him, shaking her head, and trying to focus on the task at hand. Ezekiel could still very well die if she didn't get this right. His gaze was fixed on Jasper, in some unreadable expression, so she was on her own as she pulled his arms up and pulled the bandages around the worst parts of it.

She'd watched Jasper bandage him a few weeks ago when the rookam had attacked them, and all she could do was replicate the movements he'd gone through as she used most of their bandages to cover his arms up to the elbow.

Closer inspection showed that even though the monster's claws had gone through armor, it had only managed to scratch him after doing that. So the worst injuries were to his arms, at least from what she could see.

"Not bad," Ezekiel winced, and at some point through the process, he'd looked away from Jasper and back at her. "Are you alright, Nadia?"

"It was focused on you," Nadia said, staring down at the blood on her hands. "You... probably looked like the biggest meal, between the three of us."

"Yeah."

He could have *died*. That beast... whatever it was, it had taken him so close to death so easily. They'd been too focused on Ridgeport, on getting there and then being fine... Nadia almost forgot that other people weren't the only threat.

Especially out here, they should have been keeping an eye out.

She should have been listening to the way her spine still crawled, the way she never felt safe no matter what... it was *true*, she should have been paying attention.

"What *happened*, Jasper?" Ezekiel's voice broke her from the thoughts, and he used her shoulder to try and stand on shaking legs. Nadia followed quickly, looping one arm as well as she could under his and around his torso.

"I..." Jasper had finished being sick, though he still avoided looking their way.

Whether he was ashamed of whatever this was, or he didn't want to see the blood, Nadia wasn't sure.

"What was that? What..." Ezekiel lifted a shaking hand

to point at the spike of ice, and droplets of blood from the bandages fell down, staining the earth between them. "What *are* you?"

He was angrier than Nadia had expected, while she was still swimming in confusion.

"I don't *know*."

Wind howled overhead, darkness creeping up the canyon from the valleys below, and Ezekiel swayed before leaning heavily onto Nadia's shoulder again.

"We need to find some kind of shelter." Nadia's voice seemed to work without her even trying to talk. "We- we need to start a fire, you need to *rest* Ezekiel."

"Did you *know*?" Ezekiel glared down at her, and Nadia blinked. "Did you know he- he's a caster?"

"I-I... No, I..." Jasper was a caster. Jasper could use magic this entire time. He... *what*? This didn't make any sense.

This was Jasper.

But... but no, no, he would have told her if he was a caster.

This didn't make any sense.

"You didn't know." Ezekiel sighed, shaking his head, but following her lead as she pulled him toward the base of the cliff. Jasper trailed after them, the crunching of his footsteps giving that away, and Nadia had no idea what she could even say to him, or ask him, or...

She couldn't focus on that right now.

There wasn't a true alcove or outcropping, but there was a dip into the cliff face that went all the way up, a space free of the wind and flying snow and ice where at least they could light a fire reasonably, with the wiry bushes and trees that scattered along the canyon. As long as it didn't snow too hard, the sky above wouldn't cause too many problems.

"What happened?" Ezekiel asked her, though his eyes followed Jasper as he waded wordlessly through the snow to uproot the bushes.

"I tried- I *tried*." Nadia cleared her throat and then busied herself by trying to wash the blood from her hands with the snow. "It came out of nowhere, I- my arrows barely seemed to hurt it. I don't know…"

"But you hit it, th-that's impressive." He groaned, head falling back against the rock. "And then he, what?"

"He just… screamed. And the ice exploded, I…"

"I didn't mean to." Jasper dropped his armful of wood on the ground nearby, then went to work clearing snow away. "That's never happened before."

"But you knew you were a caster," Ezekiel muttered.

It was more ire than Nadia could have ever imagined him pointing toward Jasper, she'd only ever seen fondness even in his annoyance. But this… it reminded her of the way the king would look at her when she made a mistake.

Fury, or hatred- *something*.

"I-"

"You knew you were a caster, and you never told *either* of us." Ezekiel barreled on. "Why didn't you *tell* me? What happened to *trusting* me? What happened to *knowing each other completely*? Weren't those *your* words?"

"You- you're hurt right now, you need to stay calm." Jasper returned his focus to the fire.

"*Calm?*"

"We- we can talk it out," Nadia said numbly. "But you're a- you're okay, you're alive. Right? That's what's important."

He was. He could have died- Jasper had kept this a secret, sure, but… but he'd saved Ezekiel's life. Surely Ezekiel knew that.

The soldier said nothing else, and Nadia focused on clearing more snow for the bedrolls while Jasper got a fire lit. Soon enough it was crackling as the darkness fully took the canyon, and the warmth from it coupled with her efforts got the area at least dry enough to lay out a base layer of bedrolls to sit on.

"Okay," what to do now, that there wasn't a useful task? "Okay- Jasper…"

"I don't know what that was," he still sat by the fire's edge, a few feet away from her and Ezekiel against the cliff. "It's never happened before."

"That's not the point!" Ezekiel had found his voice again, bundled in extra blankets and his cloak. "What happened to telling me everything, J? I thought.."

"I do tell you everything, but this is- this was something I *couldn't* ever say." Jasper looked over at them, eyes wide. "I wanted to tell you, both of you! But I don't even know how this works, why do you think I told you to come out here in the *first place?*"

Oh.

His insistence upon learning about Nadia's own secret made more sense, now, his excitement and research and even his confidence about magic being real in the first place.

"When- when I found out that finding a trained caster would help *you*, Nadia, I… I thought we both had a chance. I was *going* to tell you both…"

"When?" Ezekiel asked incredulously. "We're almost to Ridgeport already, Jasper, when were you planning on letting us in on this?"

"I… I don't know." Jasper curled in on himself, staring into the fire and hugging his arms tightly to his chest.

Nadia had never heard Jasper say that so many times in a day before. He usually struggled to even get the words out, in the rare instance he had to admit it.

"What, the one time it really matters and you don't have any answers?" Ezekiel asked incredulously. "Convenient."

"How was I supposed to tell you?" Jasper asked. "Magic is *illegal*, I'd be executed if anyone found out I could use it. And- and the past few weeks..."

"It's illegal because it's *dangerous*. You couldn't even control that- that- whatever it was! We're lucky you only killed the monster, and not either of *us*, you don't know what you're doing! That's why it's illegal, Jasper!"

"What, so you think I should be killed? Executed?"

"Of- no, of *course* not, don't be stupid." Ezekiel sighed. "I think you should have been honest with me like we promised."

"I-"

"If you wanted secrets, that would have been fine! I mean you shouldn't have said you told me everything when you *didn't*."

It felt almost invasive to be sitting there, listening as her only two friends in the world spit words like daggers across the fire.

"Because I did." Ezekiel continued when Jasper said nothing. "You know *everything* about me, Jasper. Because that's what *you* wanted."

"Ez, I-"

"Just- just stop. Don't..." Ezekiel grimaced as he huddled further against the bedrolls. "Don't talk to me right now."

"I'll take the first watch," Jasper whispered, turning his gaze to the flames.

"I'll take the second." Nadia agreed. *Thank the stars-*

something to do. "We'll just have two... you rest, Ezekiel."

He was asleep within only a few minutes, and part of Nadia was afraid that he would die in his sleep from the injuries, but she didn't know what else she could do for him. So she settled for sitting nearby and listening to his breath, all the while running back the past hour in her head.

This was Jasper.

She knew Jasper, she *trusted* him.

How much of his support in this was real, and how much of it was selfish?

Was it fair of her to ask that question?

Nadia didn't really know, but the question sat in the back of her head with a dozen others, cycling through confusion and wondering how on earth she could even ask, after the argument she'd just witnessed.

A good few minutes into sitting silently, Jasper stood from his watch and moved to the opening of their alcove before kneeling again to draw in the snow.

"What are-" he jumped, turning back in surprise, and Nadia laughed softly. "What are you doing?"

"I'm... *trying* to make sure nothing else can come into this space," Jasper said slowly. "I've tried it a few times, it's easier the smaller the opening. You can sleep, we'll be safe."

"Oh." The nights where he'd paced around their campsite while she and Ezekiel trained, the nights he traced words into the dust, *that's* what that had been. Restlessness, maybe, but also *magic*.

Their good luck, as they'd called it, upon not being found made more sense as well, and she watched as Jasper drew whatever it was he was drawing in the snow across the entire opening before returning to sit by the fire.

"How... you said what happened today had never happened before." She leaned to listen for Ezekiel's breath one more time, and upon hearing it she moved to sit a bit closer to the fire, and Jasper. "But how many times *have* you used it before?" How long had he been a caster?

"Magic in- in general?"

It was strange to hear him hesitate when usually Jasper would be happy to explain his studies and knowledge. She nodded, waiting for him to continue.

"On *purpose*," Jasper sighed. "Not really... before we left Dunatel. But... some of it just *happens*. I'm lucky, it mostly only affects me. That's why I'm still alive."

"What is it?" Nadia asked curiously, not content to let him be so vague. "Are you okay?"

"I can manage," Jasper said. "It- it... it's not really fair, Nadia. I try not to use it, I try to stop it when I can."

"But you've been using it since we left," Nadia gestured toward the tracings he'd left. "You've been helping us. Why didn't you-"

"I thought you'd both *hate* me." Jasper looked up at her, and his eyes held a light she didn't recognize. Jasper's gaze always held joy and curiosity, passion and intellect. This... this was something closer to the embers of the fire between them, something bright and deep and *dangerous*. "I was right. He does."

"Ezekiel doesn't-"

"Don't *lie to me!*" Jasper snapped.

"I'm not..." Nadia winced, and he just pursed his lips, proved right.

"It- it's not *fair*, Nadia. I always know when you're lying to me, I know *exactly* how you feel. Do you know how- how annoying it is to constantly feel how *everyone else feels*? Do you realize how much everyone would hate me if they knew what I knew about them? I try to ignore it, I swear to the stars I do, because it isn't *fair*."

"Wh- Jasper..." Is that what magic did? Did it give you a look inside someone's head? He'd said that only a few days ago, and she'd taken it as *speculation*.

"It's not fair, Nadia! It's not fair of me to know these things." Jasper hissed, and his voice sounded the same as the crackling fire just for a moment. "It's not fair that I always knew when you were on the edge of some kind of breakdown, but you always acted like everything was fine. It's not fair that I know you're lying right now, and it's not fair that I can *feel* how he hates me."

Nadia had never seen Jasper cry. He'd been close to it a few times recently, but now she watched tears roll down his face and freeze in the cold air.

What could she say to this? What... What could anyone say? Of *course* Jasper hadn't told them.

"It's not fair," Jasper said again, gripping his knees tightly. "But you know, now, so don't lie to me about what either of you feels."

"...I don't know how I feel," Nadia whispered. Jasper's head fell down, and he stared at the fire. "You know I mean that if you're telling the truth. It- it's just been today. I don't know how I feel about you, Jasper."

This was Jasper. Her best friend, who always acted so oblivious to everyone except for the moments when she felt desperately alone. Her best friend, who focused his life on knowledge and facts and research. Her best friend, who had been hiding this for years for the same reasons she'd been hiding how she felt about being a prince.

He was afraid.

Nadia didn't need magic to know that.

"You should sleep," Jasper said quietly. "We'll be safe, we'll get to Ridgeport tomorrow. You need rest as much as he does."

"And you don't?"

"I'll wake you at midnight, and get mine." Jasper rolled his eyes. "Go to sleep, Nadia."

This was... *Jasper*. If he said it was safe, all she could do was trust that.

Strange, telling herself such a thing didn't seem as effective now. Nadia bundled herself up anyway, next to Ezekiel again to listen to him breathe, and left Jasper to his quiet thoughtfulness by the fire.

* * *

Thanks to all the stars in the sky, Ezekiel did not die during the night. He was groggy upon waking at sunrise, and his arms shook when he tried to use them too much, but Nadia was sure there was some kind of real healer in Ridgeport that could help him better than she had.

"It's normal," he said when she asked. "I'm alive, that's what counts."

Yet he didn't so much as look at Jasper as they packed up camp, and didn't speak much at all either. It was awfully tense, Nadia was used to being quiet while they bounced between each other but now Jasper seemed resigned to the silence as well.

"Do we just leave that there?" Nadia asked before they left the camp, nodding to the now frozen body, still impaled where they'd left it. The blood had crystallized and frozen as well, both her friends had pointedly avoided looking that way.

"What would you have us do, carry it with us?" Ezekiel asked.

"I- well, I guess not." Nadia sighed. "It just feels strange to leave it like that."

Looking now, free of the adrenaline and fear, she could see the monster's bones jutting out through the fur, it looked almost emaciated. Sure, it was dead and that was probably making it look worse, but she could only imagine the beast was just looking for a meal.

The idea of Ezekiel being that meal was horrible, so she turned away and walked next to Ezekiel as he started back up the path. Jasper started off taking the rear, but after an hour or so Ezekiel's steps slowed, and if Nadia knew much more about medicine, she might be able to help or at least understand what he needed, even if they couldn't get it until they reached Ridgeport.

Either way, Jasper ended up ahead of them, a few yards or so as he kicked snow and ice out of the way as they approached a bridge. Looking forward, she could see it crossed the canyon river to a road that wound through a wider bit of it toward the pillars of smoke that must be town.

They were close, maybe closer than they thought they had been.

Ezekiel muttered a curse under his breath when he tripped, and Nadia caught him while he stumbled.

"Are you okay? Is-"

"Fine," he grit out. "Just- we just need to get there. Then I can rest and- and there'll probably be healers."

Nadia wasn't much, and she certainly wasn't a healer. Jasper at the very least had read books on the subject, but he'd been keeping his distance all morning.

"Do you want me to-"

"No." Ezekiel's gaze fell forward, tracing Jasper's movement through the snow as he made it to the bridge and knelt to inspect it.

Nadia's stomach twisted uncomfortably at the expression on his face. She couldn't quite get a read on it, but he didn't seem happy. It would probably be stranger if he seemed happy, but...

"He saved your life." She noted quietly.

"That's not what I'm upset about." Ezekiel huffed, shaking his head. "Are *you* not... he basically lied to us, spending all this time talking about finding a caster when he's *been* one. He admitted to convincing you to do this just for *his own gain*. I..."

"I'm not saying I think he's... I don't know, without fault." Nadia hardly knew how she felt, really, even after a night of thinking. "But I think he means well."

"I don't even know what to think when I look at him. I- I should focus on not dying," Ezekiel said. "And then I'll figure out what to say to *Jasper*."

"Are you sure you're alright? I don't have any more bandages, I..." she was *useless*.

"The best thing to do right now is get to an actual *place*," Ezekiel sighed as they joined Jasper at the bridge. "As far as field medicine goes, especially untrained, you did fine."

"It- it's icy," Jasper said softly. "Be careful, going across." Then he started on his own, stepping gingerly across the planks and out over the drop to an equally icy river below.

Nadia tried to ignore the dizzying drop, steadying Ezekiel as much as she could without hurting his arms while they followed.

Once across, which took not long at all but still far too much time, the path was very clearly marked with boulders and posts the way that the rest of it hadn't been. Hopefully that meant they were close, because Nadia wasn't sure how much longer she could bear the tense silence between the other two. Now that Jasper was closer to them Ezekiel was resolutely quiet.

Another hour or so passed before the path widened, opening up into a larger valley within the mountains. In the end they entered through, the nearest building was a few hundred yards away. Past that there were dozens more, winding, snow-covered streets that filled the area before a dark smudge of trees that covered the mountains past them.

A few had plumes of smoke up from the chimney, which was what they'd spotted the day before, but another stream of smoke erupted up from a crack in the northern cliff face above the village.

A simple sign on a wooden gate told Nadia what they all assumed already - they'd made it to Ridgeport.

"We're here." She was far too relieved, and Jasper was far too quiet, and Ezekiel leaned far too heavily on her shoulder. "Now what?"

To Be Continued
in
The Cursed Land - Book 2: A Magician's Soul

Glossary

Ardenia (ar-dee-nee-uh) - A country made up of three separate kingdoms, all under an alliance with each other.
 Ardenian (ar-dee-nee-ann) - A person who lives and/or is native to the country of Ardenia.

Cidon (sy-don) - The central kingdom of Ardenia.
 Cidonian (sy-don-ee-ann) - A person who was born and raised in the kingdom of Cidon.

Rasnia (Raz-nee-uh) - The most northern kingdom of Ardenia.
 Rasnian (Raz-nee-ann) - A person who was born and raised in the kingdom of Rasnia

Ashan (Ash-ann) - The most southern kingdom of Ardenia.
 Ashanian (Ash-ann-ee-ann) - A person who was born and raised in the kingdom of Ashan

Ochea (Otch-ee-uh) - A country made of islands, across the sea from Ardenia.
 Ochean (Otch-ee-ann) - A person who lives in and/or is native to the islands of Ochea

Rookam (rook-um) - A creature that lives in the swamps of Cidon.

Caster - A person who is capable of using magic

Andon (ann-don) - The Ardenian god of birth/life/new beginnings

Kaphine (Kaff-een) - The Ardenian goddess of magic

Tomera (Tow-mair-uh) - The Ardenian goddess of the sky/weather

Elbris (El-bris) - The Ardenian god of the land

Ezros (Ez-rous) - The Ardenian god of travel/travelers

Acknowledgments

I started writing this story many years ago, before I'd even gotten the chance to come out as transgender myself. Going back through and writing it now, giving Nadia the opportunity to do just that in these pages was a wonderful experience and this project has been my focus for an incredibly long time, so it's surreal to see it actually coming to life.

So first off, I'd like to thank everyone in my life who has been supportive on my journey of self-actualization - my very own versions of Jasper and Ezekiel. My Twin - Alice, is one of the warmest and kindest people I've ever known, and supports me in ways I can never thank her for. My best friends in the world - Lyric, Salem, and Fletcher, who love me for absolutely everything I am despite my (many) shortcomings. My older sister Sarah who gave me my first-ever suit (it's too small for me now, but I still have it packed away safely). Finally, all the friends and content creators on Tumblr, Twitter, Discord, and beyond who first showed me that the world isn't always black and white, and neither is gender.

Secondly, and just as important, I'd like to thank everyone in my life who put me on the path to writing. My parents, who nurtured my love of reading and writing from an incredibly young age. My Elementary school teachers, Ms. Gulledge and Mrs. Womble, who were the first to read my poems and short stories and told me to never, ever stop writing. My High school teachers, Lisa McMullin and Sam Beeson, who helped me develop voice and style and a better understanding of grammar and all the building blocks it took to get me where I am now. Writing, in a very real way, saved my life when I felt completely alone.

Special thanks to Alice once again, and our older sister Coral for being huge inspirations and showing me how they'd gone on their own journeys of self-publishing, which made this process far easier for me to step into once this story was ready.

Finally, thank you to my wonderful community of fellow fanfiction writers and readers, who have watched me grow into the storyteller I am now. It's been a very long road, and some of you have stuck with me for years and that means everything to me. Special thanks in this group to my beta-readers for this book - Zoovannah, Hatzui, DrawingAbyss, and Livon Saffron. You all helped this story become what it needed to be, and I hope you stick with me in this new era of creation - because I'm only getting started.

About the Author

I would love to be able to say that the author of this book is, in fact, an inter-dimensional seer who tells stories from other worlds. Unfortunately, that is simply not the case! Coby is just some random guy. He's never fought any mythical monsters, and he's never narrowly escaped an assassination attempt. What Coby has done, though, is spend most of his time in his own imagination wishing he could escape the real world.

Coby is transgender, and a lot of the time the real world doesn't make that easy. He found sanctuary in the world of fantasy when he was younger, and now he wants to share that sanctuary with all of you - using characters he would have loved to relate to when he was younger but didn't have access to yet. Coby brings the real into the unreal and the unreal into the real. All you have to do is open your eyes and read it.

You can connect with me on:
- https://cobythinks.net
- https://x.com/CobyThinks

Printed in the USA
CPSIA information can be obtained
at www.ICGtesting.com
LVHW041024041024
792311LV00013B/38